I0569918

A Dragon's Treasure

NYX'S PIXIE

K.M. MAHONEY

Nyx's Pixie
ISBN # 978-1-78430-417-1
©Copyright K.M. Mahoney 2015
Cover Art by Posh Gosh ©Copyright January 2015
Interior text design by Claire Siemaszkiewicz
Totally Bound Publishing

NYX'S PIXIE

Dedication

Because we can all use a little more magic in our lives.

Prologue

Nyx dodged a man in an absurd feathered hat, a woman wearing practically nothing, and one burly dwarf. He followed the narrow winding street—more of an alley, really—and tried not to snarl at the motley assortment of people and animals that kept getting in his way.

Gods, but he hated Parmouth. He would be quite content to run away and never return. If it hadn't been a direct order from his King...

Oh, do stop fooling yourself. You're here because you want to be and no other reason.

To tell the truth, if Nyx had really wanted to, he could have told Seamus to send someone else. The King would have. But there was one thing in Parmouth that couldn't be found anywhere else, and it was inside the garish building Nyx was now facing.

Nyx stood on the far side of the street and watched for a time. The occasional passing conveyance blocked his line of sight, but for the most part, he had an unobstructed view of the large wood-framed building, painted black with lurid red accents—a painfully bright sign, lit by magic, flashed the words *The Red Curtain*. He couldn't look too long at the sign—it made his head ache. The pulsing effect of the magic wasn't horrible in the sunlight afternoon, but it would be obnoxious in a few hours.

And this place is considered 'classy'.

He supposed that for a brothel, it was. The prostitutes were intelligent, articulate and, most of all, clean. The management was selective when it came to both employees and customers. You couldn't just walk in off the street and expect to spend time with one of the Curtain's courtesans. Well, you could, but you'd damn well better have deep pockets if you were going to try it. The pleasures of the Curtain didn't come cheaply.

Nyx had absolutely no interest in the majority of those pleasures. He did, however, have a deep and abiding interest in one little courtesan with deep indigo hair and mismatched eyes.

"Gods, Chaos would never cease laughing," Nyx muttered. No one looked twice at the over-sized man stalking a brothel and talking to himself—it was that sort of area.

Nyx still felt self-conscious. He tugged at his hood, pulling it farther over his dark blond hair and casting more of his sharp features into shadow. If word of this ever got back to the palace, Chaos wouldn't be the only one laughing. And he very much wanted to avoid the lecture Seamus was sure to give.

He could practically hear the sonorous tones of his leader. *You are Draak. As such, it falls to you to be a bastion of honor and dignity. The Draak do not frequent houses of pleasure.*

And then Raven would join in, and Nyx would be forced to listen to even more lessons in behavior. It was infuriating, especially as he seemed to be the only one subjected to said lessons. When Kirit had set fire to the West Wing, Seamus had laughed. When Chaos had humiliated an Eastern ambassador, he'd simply been sent North for a few weeks to help wage battle on the Demon Lords—hardly much of a punishment, since Chaos was disturbingly fond of a good fight.

But if Nyx stepped one toe out of line, he was chided and lectured until his ears began to buzz. And if Seamus ever found out how much time he had been spending in the red light district of Parmouth...well, the sermonizing would never cease.

A small shape flitted around the side of the building and caught Nyx's attention. He straightened from his slouch against the nearest wall and narrowed his eyes. His better-than-average eyesight was able to make out a tiny form, laden with packages and a very large basket, delicately picking its way down the refuse-strewn alley.

Every one of his considerable senses went on high alert. Nyx realized his mouth was open, forked tongue hanging out, the better to catch scent. He snapped his jaw closed, but couldn't peel his eyes from the small man.

The figure stepped around the building and began to walk quickly down the street. His filmy loose pants and tight shirt, open to the waist, did little to conceal his body. Nyx resisted the urge to whip off his cloak and cover the tiny man. No one should be looking but Nyx. No one. Ever.

As if sensing he was under observation, the man stopped in the middle of the street, cocking his head and looking around. Nyx slunk deeper into the shadows. After a moment, the man shrugged and began walking again.

Nyx waited for a few moments. Then, feeling very much like a stalker, he began trailing the man in the direction of the marketplace.

Chapter One

The big man was back.

Pol stared, mouth suddenly dry, as the door opened to admit the epitome of masculinity. Wide shoulders barely fit through the entrance, and he had to duck his head to clear the lintel. Pol started to pant. He instinctively moved the tray to cover his burgeoning erection, ridiculously obvious in his thin trousers.

Unfortunately, he forgot that the tray was fully loaded.

A loud crash echoed through the room, pottery scattering in a wide pattern across the floor.

Pol froze, heart pounding now for a different reason, and stared at the mess at his feet. *Oh, shit.*

Enid was heading his direction, a dark scowl on her face. He wanted to tell her the expression marred her pretty features in a decidedly unattractive way, but he was in enough trouble. This made the third tray he'd dropped this week.

He couldn't help it. Pol knew he'd been distracted and clumsy but he simply couldn't focus. Especially not with *him* in the room.

"Pol!"

Pol cringed and returned to staring at his feet. "Sorry, Mistress," he muttered.

"Why do I put up with you?" she ranted.

Because you have to. He didn't say that, either. It wouldn't do to remind Enid that, for all she liked to pretend, she wasn't actually in charge of the business. That would be Jamal, and Jamal had a soft spot for Pol.

Without a word, Pol dropped to his knees and began picking up the shattered remains of plates, cups and one large teapot. Customers and employees alike averted their eyes, and he sighed in relief.

Pol hated being the center of attention.

He finished mopping up puddles before grabbing his tray and scurrying back to the kitchen. The cook, a big burly man with a gruff demeanor, was waiting for him with a new tray laden with a new tea service.

"Don't drop this one," he ordered.

Pol nodded and swapped burdens. He scurried back out as fast as he'd come, eager to escape. It was annoying — out front, he had Enid glaring at him. In back, he had Septimus. Neither one was exactly brimming with sunshine and light.

Pol dutifully made the rounds, refilling pots, passing out plates of delicate hors d'oeuvres, and trying his best to remain unnoticed. He couldn't stop himself from sneaking glances. The big man still stood just inside the entrance, arms crossed over his wide chest, surveying the room with an arrogance bred into his very bones. He didn't seem to notice Pol, but then no one ever did. The hired help in a place like this was an invisible fixture, particularly one with his size — or lack of size, as the case may be.

Immediate duties completed, Pol went back to his post at the far edge of the room. He clutched his still half-full tray and waited for someone to need something. It was boring, but it was his job. Although, it was sometimes fun to observe the people. Tonight, he couldn't pry his gaze from the new arrival. The occasional person approached the man, but he sent them all away quite quickly, sometimes with nothing more than a hard stare. It made Pol absurdly happy every time one of the working men and women turned away in failure.

It was business as usual at the Curtain tonight. Women and men flirted, conversed and struck deals, mostly of a carnal nature. That was, after all, what this place was for.

The Red Curtain was one of the biggest and best brothels on the entire Western coast. It catered to the upper classes—these were not street-corner whores. The men and women who worked here wore silk and satin, spoke in well-modulated tones, and could converse easily about subjects covering politics to literature and everything in between. They made enough in one night to be picky—the clients had to work to gain the attention of one of the Curtain's courtesans. Making it through the front door didn't guarantee anything, and that was hard enough to do on its own. The management at the Curtain was even pickier than the courtesans.

And then there was Pol. Little, plain, stuck somewhere between upstairs and downstairs. His lineage was too good, elevating him above the status of most of the servants, but it wasn't good enough to get him to the next level. Maybe if he'd been pretty or charming, or anything but what he was. No one was going to pay to bed a shy, naïve little half-pixie. Pol figured he should be lucky that Jamal had known his parents and was willing to take pity on him. Mostly, Pol found it hard to summon up the appropriate gratitude.

He wanted more out of life than pouring tea and hiding in corners. Unfortunately, that had been his lot for nearly two years, and he didn't see it changing anytime soon. There simply wasn't much out there for someone like him.

A noble dressed in flashy clothes and sporting a ring worth more than Pol's entire life waved him over. Pol refilled the teapot then retreated again. The move had taken him closer to the front of the room. Pol ducked back behind a curtain, staring with wide eyes at the broad shoulders and the heart-stopping features of the man he had dreamed of every night for the last month. Lately, the dreams had begun invading Pol's waking hours as well, contributing heavily to his absent-minded behavior and his new tendency to drop everything.

Thick hair, dark in the dim and smoke-filled room, hung in a ponytail draping halfway down his back. Three loose braids hung beside his narrow face. Some people would say the man wasn't all that handsome. His eyes were dark and narrow, nose large and sharp. Scars littered his cheeks with barely visible white lines. His upper body bulged with muscles, arms nearly as thick as most men's thighs.

Pol thought he was the most gorgeous sight in the world.

Safe in his hiding place, Pol could study the stranger to his heart's content, at least until the next time he was summoned. He managed a solid five minutes of voyeurism before a flash of red made him spring back into action.

Jamal strode into the room with the confidence of a man in his element. His dark skin gleamed under the low gaslight, a stunning contrast to the deep red of his robes — Jamal would never be caught wearing any other color. He went directly to the intimidating man with a welcoming smile.

Pol began edging around the room, trying to get closer. When he did, he shamelessly eavesdropped.

"Nyx, twice in one month? The king must not be keeping you busy enough."

"Don't tell him that," the man said, flashing a smile that was all pointed teeth.

Nyx. Pol felt a little thrill at having a name to go with the face. The deep voice caused his gut to clench, and Pol nearly dropped his tray again.

"I have been watching. Not interested in a playmate tonight?" Jamal pressed. He ran one finger down Nyx's arm, and Pol had to fight against a strange surge of jealousy.

"Perhaps, if it were the right playmate." Nyx cocked his head and raised one eyebrow, his smile turning more than a little predatory.

"Come to my office." Jamal's teeth gleamed brightly against his skin. The owner was stunning and he knew it. "We can discuss your…requirements."

Pol clutched the edges of his tray until his knuckles turned white. *No, no, no.*

Despite his inner chant, he could do nothing but watch as Nyx followed Jamal from the room.

* * * *

Jamal was an attractive man and at any other time, Nyx would have quite happily taken him up on the not-so-subtle offer. With the little courtesan's gaze burning a hole in his back, though, Nyx could barely summon up a flicker of arousal for the owner of the Red Curtain.

The man had Pixie in him—that much Nyx knew. He was tiny. Really, teeny tiny. Maybe five three, tops. His features were delicate, almost androgynous, his body lithe and slender. Hell, even the man's feet were delicate.

He had watched the small man hovering near the wall, eyes on the floor. Every so often something would make that pretty mouth twitch up in a smile, but he didn't mingle like the others.

His mate.

Small, pretty and shy. Yes, definitely Pixie. His deep indigo hair and mismatched eyes proclaimed his half-breed status, more than explanation enough for his presence in Parmouth. Some races did not react well to mixed offspring, and the Pixies were one of them.

Personally, Nyx thought they were all idiots. He had never seen anything quite as stunning as those eyes, one pale green and one pale blue. They reminded him of spring.

And now I sound like a love-sick sap. Next thing you know, I'll be writing sonnets. And no one wants that, I'm a lousy poet.

Nyx stepped into Jamal's office, closing the door behind him. The room was warm and comfortable, more of a sitting area than a place to conduct business. But then again, Jamal's type of business was better handled in comfort. Nyx settled his over-sized bulk onto a delicate sofa and prayed it would hold. He really hated this new trend for fancily carved furniture with spindly legs. He never trusted it to withstand his not-inconsiderable weight.

Jamal smirked at Nyx's obvious discomfort. Now that they were alone, he dropped the seductive mask and became brisk and sensible.

"Tea?" he offered. "Or...no, I think something stronger tonight, yes?"

Nyx didn't bother to respond, but he did accept the snifter of brandy with a nod. He sipped at the heady alcohol and waited with ill-concealed patience. He knew from experience that it was best to let Jamal open the negotiations. Otherwise, the man made things difficult.

"So, someone in particular has caught your eye." Jamal's smile was more than a little smug. "Might I ask what morsel appeals to our most illustrious patron?"

"Shut up, Jamal," Nyx retorted bluntly.

Jamal sighed dramatically. "Draak. Always so blunt. No appreciation for subtlety."

"We leave that to the Fae. They do it so well."

Jamal chuckled. He used one be-ringed hand to push the silky fall of his dark hair back, revealing the tip of one extremely pointed ear. "I cannot argue with you. We do have an absurd fondness for subterfuge."

"And you never say what you mean. It's extremely annoying."

"Oh, very well, if you insist. So, who do you want and for how long?"

"The little Pixie. And I don't intend to give him back."

Jamal's black eyes widened and he blinked rapidly several times. Nyx looked on in amazement, having never seen quite that reaction from the man.

"The pixie isn't for rent," Jamal said. His earlier mellifluous tone vanished under the hard, flat speech of a man who was dangerous to cross.

"He's here, isn't he?" Nyx scowled, flashing his fangs in warning. He was dangerous, too. And he could bite quite a bit more viciously than any damned Fae.

"Just because he works here doesn't mean he's a courtesan, you damned dragon." Jamal glared at Nyx with narrowed eyes. "Pick someone else."

"No."

"You can't have him."

"Care to wager on that?"

"Damn it, Nyx!"

Nyx smirked and finished off his brandy. It was quite good, but then, he expected nothing less of Jamal.

Jamal sat back in his chair and dragged one his hand over his face. "Pol does *not* serve patrons, and I'm not going to make an exception for you."

Pol. Nyx finally had a name. He knew his smile was on the sappy side, but he couldn't seem to help it.

"Oh, by the Gods, he's a potential mate, isn't he?"

Nyx kept silent, but he did bare his teeth. Let Jamal make of that what he would.

Jamal stood abruptly and began pacing. He muttered to himself furiously in Westren. Nyx didn't bother trying to follow the patter of words. His Westren was shaky, at best. The words weren't really aimed at him, anyway.

Nyx spent several entertaining moments watching an uncharacteristically flustered Jamal traverse the room. Eventually, the man slowed then stopped in front of Nyx. Jamal planted his hands on his hips and heaved a breath of annoyance.

"Mate."

Nyx cocked his head.

"Damn it. Very well, I will speak with Pol. But that is *all* I will do. The rest is up to you. I guarantee nothing."

Nyx nodded. "I accept your offer."

Jamal nodded back, extending his hand. They clasped, sealing the tentative deal. "Wait here."

Nyx agreed wordlessly, settling back in the couch to wait.

"Oh, and, Nyx?"

"Hmm?"

"I'm fond of the boy. Do anything to harm him, and I will be very displeased. Understood?"

"What part of potential mate don't you understand?" Nyx grumbled.

"The part where you're infallible. Screw this up, and I'll remove your balls."

"Very nice," Nyx replied with an approving nod. "A threat worthy of a Draak."

Jamal threw his hands up in exasperation and left, grousing about dragons in general.

Nyx just smiled. It wasn't anything he hadn't heard before. Dragons tended to irritate people. He would prefer them terrified, but annoyed worked, too.

Chapter Two

"Pol!"

Pol jumped, which was not the best idea, considering he was crouched on the floor at the time. He toppled over and landed on his butt on the hard stone floor.

Ouch.

At least he had a decent amount of padding back there. For a little guy, he'd been told he had an overly generous arse. He was small, but rounded, which had caused more than one person to mistake him for a woman from behind.

He was rather used to it.

Pol clambered to his feet to stand before Jamal, eyes fastened to the floor. Jamal clucked his tongue, and Pol knew he was shaking his head.

"Oh, Pol, what are we going to do with you?"

I am what I am. Pol shrugged.

"Never mind." Jamal waved his hand dismissively. "Walk with me, lovely."

Pol fell into step. One didn't disobey a command from Jamal—not if one wanted to stay employed.

Jamal stayed quiet as they traversed the narrow hallways of the old building. They passed from the public areas, all gilt and glamour, and into the more practical ones, the back corridors used by the servants and courtesans, which were barren and plain. Then they went even further, out a side entrance and along the path to the gardens.

Any self-respecting brothel these days boasted a garden, the larger and more ornate, the better. Several of the more popular poets had adopted a trend of...well, outdoor seduction, Pol supposed you could call it. Lots of odes sung to ladies under the moonlight and amongst the fragrant rosebuds. That sort of nonsense. The words were pretty, but they didn't always make a lot of sense in their configuration.

Pol wasn't a big fan of poetry. At least, not *spoken* poetry. *Lyrics, on the other hand...*

"I have a...dilemma," Jamal said, breaking into Pol's random musings, for which Pol was almost thankful. "A most unusual one."

Not knowing how he was supposed to respond to that, Pol kept silent. He stopped when Jamal stopped, under the spreading limbs of an old oak, and scuffed the toe of his soft slippers against the crushed rock path.

"Oh, do look at me, Pol," Jamal ordered.

Pol looked up reluctantly. Jamal smiled, the expression gentle. "That's better. Now, I need you to listen. There is, at this moment, a very large dragon in my office."

"Dragon!" Pol's cheeks reddened at the way the word squeaked at the end, but...*dragon*. "How did it fit?"

"No, no," Jamal said, laughing. "Draak. Dragon shifter. I assure you, he's entirely human at the moment. Although, he does still take up more than his fair share of the room."

"Oh. Oh!" *Nyx. The big, gorgeous, dream-inspiring* —

"Yes. Oh."

"Don't... I mean, what is a Draak doing here?" The dragons were the king's personal retinue. Everyone knew that. As far as Pol was aware, they split their time between the capital of Aleusia and the mountains they claimed as their own. They rarely ventured this far west, unless on royal business. In which case, Pol highly doubted they would be visiting a house of pleasure.

"That is where my dilemma comes. You see, he has come because of you."

"Me?" And there was that damnable squeak again. Curse his Pixie genetics — his voice was taking years to settle, rather than months. It didn't help that the average age of maturity for a pixie was a lot higher than most races. To a pixie, anything under fifty was still a child, and Pol was only twenty-two.

"Yes, you. Lord Nyx says you are a potential consort for him — a mate, in the dragon's vernacular. Considering how seriously dragons take their mates, I am inclined to believe him."

"A mate?" Pol was beginning to feel ridiculous, as all he could seem to do was parrot Jamal's words. They just sounded so far-fetched, though. *Me? A dragon's consort?*

"Mates are touchy things," Jamal continued. "While fate can match two people, it is not a guarantee of a successful relationship. Lord Nyx would like the opportunity to get to know you, to see if your compatibility will translate into a deeper bond."

So far, Pol wasn't seeing a downside. *Spend time with the mouth-watering dragon? No, not seeing any downside at all.*

"I would be less concerned if the courting took place here, where I could supervise. A Draak, however, has duties, ones which I would never ask him to neglect. It is necessary for him to return to Aleusia. You would need to accompany him."

"I... He is a good man?" Pol asked. "You trust him?"

Jamal sighed. "I do," he admitted, albeit reluctantly. "The Draak are, on the whole, honorable men. You could not do better. I simply... Well, you mean a great deal to me, Pol."

Jamal turned to face him. His dark eyes were sad as he reached out to brush a lock of hair from Pol's eyes. "You look so much like your parents."

Pol could feel the grief, both his own and Jamal's, still so strong even after several years. He didn't know for certain what Jamal had been to his parents, but he had always sensed that the bond went far beyond mere friendship.

"I have failed you in so many ways," Jamal continued with a heavy sigh.

"No, you've—"

"I have. I should have been able to do more than give you a menial position in a whorehouse."

"You've given me a place," Pol argued. "It was certainly better than living in the streets."

"Your father would be furious with me. I should have done more to help secure your birthright."

"There was nothing you could do, and you know it." Pol's voice was bitter, but he hated thinking about that time of his life. "It's in the past, and I would prefer to leave it there."

"Yes, which is why, despite what I told Lord Nyx, I'm going to encourage you to take his offer. There is no future for you here, lovely. But perhaps, with the Draak, you can regain some of what you have lost."

I would just be happy with a home. That was what Pol missed most. Not the luxuries or the privilege, but the laughter and warmth. The security of knowing there was someone there who cared. Knowing he was loved. Oh, Jamal cared in his own way, but it wasn't the same. His love had gone to Pol's mother and father—there wasn't much left over for their only offspring. He had played the part of doting uncle to an extent but he wasn't, on the whole, a caring man.

"Could…? Would I be able to speak with him first? Perhaps…a dinner?"

"Oh, what a marvelous idea." Jamal clapped his hands, his grin suddenly turning incandescent. "I will have the staff lay a meal in the third parlor. You and the handsome dragon can get to know each other."

Jamal whirled in a swirl of heavy fabric, robes swinging around his legs. He rushed off, attention already on whatever plans he was hatching.

"Oh, Goddess, what did I do?" Pol murmured. He was amused, though. Jamal was never happier than when he had a project.

Pol just hoped the man didn't go overboard.

* * * *

Nyx waited with impatience for Jamal to return, but the blasted man never showed. After waiting an inordinate amount of time—all right, so maybe it was only five minutes—Nyx went searching. Now that he had finally decided to pursue his mate, Nyx found he was completely unwilling to wait any longer.

He waylaid three different people before someone could point him in the right direction. Nyx almost sighed in relief. The people here were uncomfortably clingy. They kept touching him, and it made his skin itch. Of course, that could be his scales. A thin layer of his dark dragon skin was popping up along his arms, a sure sign that he was nervous. Nyx tugged at his sleeves, then immediately felt silly. He was wearing a long-sleeved tunic. And if someone could see through his clothing, Nyx had more to worry about than a few scales.

"One left, two rights, third door," Nyx muttered. "Damn, this place is a worse maze than the palace. Was it the first left or the second?"

"The door on the end."

Nyx turned to see the servant who had given him directions, head poking around the last corner, a smirk on his face.

"The end?"

"Uh uh. Left through there, then the two rights. Just listen for the yelling."

"The yelling?" Nyx said to himself, already walking away. "He had better not be yelling at my ma—"

Nyx was cut off when the door that was his destination suddenly flew open. He had to take a step back to keep from getting smashed in the face.

"Careful," he snarled.

"Oh, I beg your pardon." Jamal stood there, a smile on his face. Nyx couldn't help but notice that the expression wasn't the slightest bit apologetic. Instead, Jamal seemed amused. *Damn the man.*

"Couldn't wait, hmm?"

Nyx didn't bother to dignify that with a reply. His attempt at snootiness, unfortunately, didn't affect Jamal's smirk.

"This way, my lord. I've had a small meal prepared in a private room so you and Pol could talk."

Talk. Nyx wrinkled his nose. He wasn't as taciturn as his clutch-mate Kirit, but Nyx could think of a number of things he would rather do than talk. Particularly with his mate.

Nyx licked his lips.

"Stop that," Jamal scolded. "You will have a conversation, and nothing more. A *verbal* one," Jamal stressed. Nyx realized he was leering and tried to school his features.

It was hard. They were closer now, and he couldn't stop his nose from twitching. He tilted his head back, inhaling deeply. Buried under the smells of perfume, incense and roasted meat was a tantalizing aroma. Fresh, earthy, like a garden at midnight.

His mate. Nyx had to swallow a rumble. *Civilized. I have to be civilized.* Even if all he wanted to do was jump the owner of that smell and lick him from head to foot. In all his many years, Nyx had only come across one potential mate before. It was decades ago — Nyx avoided thinking about how many — and he hadn't reacted like this. The need hadn't been nearly this strong. That particular potential had already belonged to another, a fact Nyx hadn't lamented too much at the time. He had been young and not really ready to settle down with one person. But as the years had dragged on and no one else had shown up, he had begun regretting letting that one go.

He wasn't regretting it now.

"Here we are." Jamal threw a door open with a flourish. Nyx berated himself for letting his attention wander — he had no clue where he was, and even less of an idea how to get back to the front door. Oh, well, he'd worry about it later.

Nyx stepped into the room, any and all worries fleeing. He stared in open-mouthed disbelief. "Good grief…"

The place was…well, it was something. What, he didn't know. He was too busy trying to clear the spots from his eyes. He had no idea anyone could get that much light from candles. Of course, there were probably close to a thousand, and how the hell had they got them all lit? They covered every single surface, and most of said surfaces were gilded and carved. The light reflected off the gold patina on the furniture, the sparkle equal to any dragon's hoard, just not as pretty. There was something fake about it. *Of course there is, it is fake.* Gold plate was never as shiny as real gold, and the dull gleam didn't excite him like the real thing.

Jamal had probably been aiming for romantic, but it was mostly just gaudy.

"Enjoy your dinner." Jamal backed out of the room and pulled the door closed, but Nyx could still feel eyes on him. *Blasted brothel and their blasted peepholes.*

Another door opened, a curtain shifted, and Pol came into view. Immediately, Nyx forgot about everything. Pol was prettier than any glitter, prettier than anything Nyx had in his hoard.

Prettier than anything Nyx had ever seen, including that dagger of Raven's with the jeweled hilt that Nyx had coveted for damn near fifty years.

"Hello, little one." Nyx's voice came out in a low rumble, almost down in the inaudible-to-humans range—or Pixies. Or… *Shit, not even my mental ramblings are making sense. What is it about this man?*

"Hello."

Oh. Oh, that voice.

Nyx could listen to the little Pixie speak all day. One word was all, but it sent shivers of lust up Nyx's spine. He had never heard such a smooth, musical tenor.

"Come, sit," Nyx urged.

"Let me just… It's very bright in here." Pol walked the edges of the room, carefully extinguishing some of the candles.

"It is rather excessive."

"Jamal delights in excess."

"I don't want to talk about Jamal."

"No?"

Nyx shook his head. "No."

Pol cocked his head, looking very much like a dragon for an instant. Albeit a very tiny dragon. "What do you want to talk about?"

"You."

Nyx watched in fascination as Pol blushed. The bright red was a beautiful contrast against his creamy skin. He wanted to touch, to feel the heat.

"We should…" Pol gestured to the low table that took up the center of the room. Nyx absently followed the suggestion, seating himself on one of the large cushions. He never looked away from Pol.

Pol blushed again before settling across from Nyx at the table. It was long and narrow, leaving them separated by mere feet.

The instant Pol's delightfully curved arse hit the cushion, several servants appeared.

Oh, yes, we are definitely being watched. It made Nyx growly, but he shoved his aggressive side down. He wanted to woo the little man, not scare him. *No, no, don't scare him, or he'll never agree to come home with you.*

And Nyx wanted that, more than anything. It would be a challenge. He would have to be *charming*.

28

Damn, I hope I'm up to it.

Nyx hadn't needed to be charming in... Well, he couldn't remember the last time. He wasn't a vain man, but the dragons were held in high regard and viewed with awe by more than a few people. It wasn't a boast to say he never had problems finding someone to share his bed. He had just never found anyone he wanted to keep for more than a couple of nights. And if the person he tried to lure to his room wasn't interested, there was always someone to take their place.

With Pol, it mattered. No one else would do. And Nyx had the sinking feeling in the pit of his stomach that no one else would ever do again.

Pol leaned to one side to let Anson put down a platter of meat. It was still sizzling, the smell making his mouth water—he hadn't been able to eat yet this evening. Even while the food was calling to him, though, Pol could feel the piercing eyes of a dragon boring into him. He didn't think Nyx had looked away once since Pol had come into the room.

Pol licked his lips, feeling rather like a rabbit being stalked by a hawk. Like prey.

It was rather thrilling. No one had ever looked at him like that before.

Pol waited for the others to leave before he began to silently serve the food. He bit his lower lip, trying desperately to think of things to say. As usual, his mind remained blank. Polite conversation was not his specialty.

He finished filling Nyx's plate with food, the service automatic. It felt right, to take care of the man this way. Nyx smiled and thanked him.

Pol couldn't help noticing the abundance of sharp teeth in that smile. It made him shiver, although he didn't think it was with fear.

They ate quietly for several moments. Pol could hear the clock on the other side of the room ticking. The silence was awkward and heavy.

Pol had never hated his shy nature more.

"Have you worked here long?" Nyx asked. There was a note of distaste to his voice.

"A few years. Jamal was a friend of my parents. After they died, he gave me a place."

"Generous of him." The sarcasm was thick, but Pol chose to pretend he didn't hear it.

He shrugged one shoulder. "It isn't a bad place to work. I serve the guests, assist the cook when needed. Most people leave me alone."

"They had better keep it that way."

Jealous already? That was a good sign, wasn't it?

"You... Jamal says you work for the king? I admit, I don't know much about the dragons. They...you...don't come this far west very often."

"There is usually not much need for us in this area. The trading keeps most factions friendly enough, and the militia is well equipped to handle the problems that do arise. Occasionally, however, the king feels the need to remind the fringes of his empire of our presence."

"There are a lot of dragons, then?"

"No, only four. Raven is our leader, Kirit his second. Then myself and Chaos. We serve as the king's right arm, but we are not as in demand as we used to be. We are warriors, and Faerie has been peaceful for a long time, now."

"I suppose." Pol stabbed at his vegetables, searching for another topic, since Nyx seemed to be done with that one. Nyx, for his part, appeared enamored with his meat, although Pol could still feel his penetrating gaze at times.

"Are all the others mated?" There, that was a decent discussion that might lead to what Pol really wanted to know.

"Only Kirit. He mated last year, to a human from Earth."

"Really?" Pol asked in surprise. "I don't believe I've ever met a human. One that wasn't born here, that is."

"Cody is…well, he's Cody. Let's just leave it at that."

Pol furrowed his brow, confused, but let it go. More silence, grating along his spine. Pol could feel a headache coming, probably from racking his brain. *Damn it, I* hate *making small talk.*

He wished Nyx would just jump over the table and claim him. Take the choice away. Although, not really, because if asked, Pol had already decided. He wanted this dragon, and not just because he was the most handsome man Pol had ever seen. It was something more, something deeper. Nyx called to him at every level, and the thought of never seeing the big dragon again made his chest ache.

"Would—"

"Will you come to Aleusia with me?" Nyx blurted out abruptly.

Pol closed his mouth and blinked a few times before the words registered. "I…with you? As, what?"

"My mate. You are my mate. I need to return to the capital in the morning, but I do not wish to leave you behind. So, will you accompany me?"

Pol swallowed, then grabbed his wine glass to soothe his suddenly dry mouth. This was what he wanted, wasn't it?

Nyx stood and rounded the table. He pulled Pol up beside him. Pol knew his mouth was probably gaping, but damn. He hadn't realized how huge Nyx was. Pol barely reached his shoulder.

Then Nyx cradled Pol's face in his hands. He leaned down, brushing his lips across Pol's, and Pol's mind went completely and utterly blank. He returned the pressure tentatively, not quite certain what he was supposed to do. He'd seen people kissing, of course, but he'd never been on the receiving end.

Nyx moved his hands, one going to cup the back of Pol's neck, the other resting at the small of his back. He pulled Pol in close, deepening the kiss. His tongue prodded at Pol's lips with gentle but insistent force, until Pol slowly opened his mouth. Nyx's tongue surged inside, tangling with Pol's. The kiss grew harder, and Pol moaned into Nyx's mouth. Nyx tilted his head, their lips meeting and parting. His hands tightened on Pol, and Pol clutched at Nyx's shoulders like he never wanted to let go.

Pol shivered, lust stringing his body taut. He ached with need, his penis throbbing. He needed more, needed…something. Pol made a sound of frustration, trying to get closer to Nyx. To his extreme displeasure, Nyx gentled the kiss, pulling back slightly. His tongue merely dipped now, tracing along Pol's lips, but no longer trying to explore the recesses of his mouth.

"No," Pol murmured, tugging at the dark red cloth of Nyx's tunic. "More."

"Shhh, little one," Nyx said. He trailed his lips along Pol's cheek and down, nuzzling the base of his neck. He nipped lightly at the spot where Pol's neck and shoulder met, and Pol shuddered violently.

"Oh," he gasped. "There. I need—"

"Easy." Nyx pressed one last kiss to the spot and pulled away. Pol wanted to yank him closer and climb him like a tree, but he couldn't get the big body to budge. It was like trying to shift a boulder.

"Nyx," he pleaded, even though he wasn't quite certain what he was pleading for.

"Hush. Not here, not now." Nyx brushed a strand of bright hair away from Pol's face. "We are being watched."

Pol scowled. "I'm going to kick Jamal in the shin."

Nyx laughed, the sound deep. It hit Pol in the gut, sending another shiver up his spine, and made his cock harden even more. He wanted to hear it again.

"I would like to see that, little one. But for now, perhaps we should finish our meal, yes?"

"I suppose." The food didn't really appeal to Pol anymore. He was still hungry, but it was a different kind of hungry. He wanted Nyx, not food.

Unfortunately, Nyx seemed intent on being the epitome of chivalry. He helped Pol take a seat before resuming his own place at the table. They made small talk, although Pol wouldn't be able to say what they discussed. He was too busy squirming on the cushion. He needed relief, desperately. He pushed the food around on his plate, pretending to eat. Pretending to be fascinated with Nyx's words.

In reality, while he listened, he focused mainly on the deep rumble of Nyx's voice and the musky smell of the dragon's skin.

It was the longest meal of Pol's life. When Nyx stood again, Pol barely suppressed a cheer.

Nyx took Pol's hand, but didn't draw him any closer. There was strain showing around the dragon's dark green eyes, and Pol took perverse delight in that. At least he wasn't the only one suffering.

"I can feel Jamal's impatience," Nyx said with a small smile. "So I believe it is time I took my leave. I won't press you for an answer tonight."

Nyx placed one hand on Pol's jaw, caressing Pol's skin with his thumb. "Dream of me, little one. And if you decide being a dragon's mate is what you want, be ready to leave two hours after dawn. I will come for you."

He dropped his hand with what Pol thought was reluctance. After one last long look, Nyx turned and left. Pol stared at the empty space in front of him. He whimpered, wanting to call the dragon back.

But Nyx was right. Pol needed to give this more than the brief amount of thought he'd already spared. While every inch of him was crying out to say yes, it would mean huge changes. The attraction was strong, but was it worth leaving everything and everyone he knew behind?

He suspected it was. Pol touched his lips, remembering that kiss. *Oh, yes, I do think it will be worth it.*

Pol slipped from the room, taking the back way in an attempt to avoid Jamal. Jamal would find him eventually, but Pol needed to mull things over in his head for a bit.

Then he needed to pack.

Chapter Three

The bang reverberated with stunning force through the room. Cody winced. He'd found out quickly that things echoed horribly in the stone halls of his new home. And with the twisty, convoluted configuration of tunnels, he never could tell quite where the sound was coming from.

Except this time, he thought he knew.

"What the hell, Kirit?" he bellowed, shoving aside the curtain that separated the bedroom and the living space. "It's not even dawn. I was trying to sleep! I thought you weren't coming back until tomorrow."

His dragon stood just inside their front door, scowling ferociously. He was growling, the sound low, ominous and damn near continuous. A small cloud of smoke nearly obscured his narrow features.

"What has you so worked up?" Cody demanded, coming to a quick stop.

"Seamus." The word was nearly incomprehensible, wrapped as it was in a dull roar.

"Of course." It was always about Seamus. Sometimes, Cody wanted nothing more than to shove the damned fairy off a convenient cliff. Unfortunately, since Seamus was the king of the Fae, that particular action would have consequences Cody really didn't want to deal with. "What has His Supreme Majesty done now?"

Kirit just snarled.

Cody sighed. "We've talked about this, big guy. Words. I need words, remember?" He'd gotten pretty good at interpreting Kirit's vast range of vocalizations, but he couldn't read minds. Not yet, anyway. He needed to check and see if Linria had made any progress on that spell.

Cody made for the small sitting area in one corner of the large room, plopping down onto a pile of round squishy pillows. He patted the space next to him. "Come here, big guy, and tell me all about it."

Kirit didn't lose any of his anger, but he did follow Cody's not-so-gentle suggestion.

Kirit slumped down, propping his head on his fist. Under the anger, Cody could see a distinct pout forming. He really wished they had cameras in Faerie. Kirit kept insisting that dragons didn't pout—Cody would love to be able to prove otherwise.

Cody leaned close and ran his fingers through Kirit's loose, waist-length hair. The dark color shimmered, flashing with blues and reds in the low light.

"Talk to me," he coaxed.

Kirit sighed and lay on his back, staring blankly at the ceiling. "I suppose it is not truly Seamus' fault. Not this time. But he says we can no longer delay The Renewal."

"Okay, what's The Renewal?" Cody drawled the word. The way Kirit said it, he could practically see the capital letters.

"It is a long, involved spell in which the dragons participate."

"Not seeing the problem."

"It takes two months."

"I'll come with you."

"In seclusion."

"What?" Cody wasn't liking the sound of this so much now. It had been over a year since they'd mated, and in all that time, they had never been apart for more than one night. Kirit would, on occasion, need to go to the palace, and he refused to allow Cody to accompany him. He'd been touchy ever since that whole incident with the king's cousin.

Honestly, it had only been a few bruises—and the man was dead. Kirit really needed to let it go.

Dragons were nothing if not stubborn.

"What is this spell for, and is there any way to get out of it?"

Kirit shook his head, and Cody's hopes sank. "As much as I would will it otherwise, the spell is necessary."

"Explain it to me. You keep circling the subject, and it's getting annoying."

"Once every hundred years, the dragons are put into a deep sleep. Seamus casts a spell over us, and while we slumber, it adjusts our magic."

"Great, so you get to sleep for two months and I do…what?"

"I don't know, mate!" Kirit burst out, his frustration a palpable force.

It took Cody by surprise and he blinked for a minute. Then he asked the question that he probably should have started with. "What happens if you don't do it?"

Kirit appeared reluctant to speak. "Us, my clutch, we are…not quite right."

"What does that mean?"

"Remember what I told you? About Artemis and Sciota?"

Cody had to think about it for a minute, then an almost-forgotten conversation floated through his mind. When they'd first come to the dragonlands— Benndragos, as Kirit called it—Kirit had told him a story about Artemis and Sciota, the last pure dragons. Sciota had died and Artemis had pined away without her mate, eventually disappearing without a trace. With their loss, pure dragons had vanished from Faerie.

"You mean about how Seamus makes the dragon eggs out of magic and a male dragon fertilizes them? You know, about that, if the two dragons were both gone, then who fertilized the first egg?"

Kirit stared. "That is irrelevant."

Cody took it to mean Kirit didn't know.

"The point," Kirit continued, "is that the current dragons are not real dragons. We are not as nature intended. We need a spell periodically to renew our magic and keep our essence intact."

Cody was starting to grow exasperated with the big lug—not a new experience. "So I ask again. What. Happens?"

"We lose our ability to change."

Cody cursed. "So you can't become a dragon anymore?"

Kirit shook his head again. "Our dragon is our primary form. We can no longer become human."

"Well, fuck!" Cody stood and began tugging at the massive supine form at his feet. "Let's go. I'm not risking that!"

Among other things, he couldn't have sex with a dragon. And Kirit wouldn't fit in their bedroom anymore, or through their front door, or...hell. It would just be *wrong*.

Kirit resisted all efforts to get him off the floor. He pulled, and Cody landed on top of the large chest. He gasped as the impact knocked the breath out of his lungs. Kirit was *not* soft anywhere, Cody noted, squirming a little.

"Horny bastard," he said with a laugh.

"Always," Kirit replied matter-of-factly. He reached up and stole a kiss, which Cody eagerly returned.

Gods above, he loved kissing his mate. He would never grow tired of the way Kirit tasted, or the way he did that thing with his tongue.

Cody hummed with happiness, sliding his own tongue along Kirit's. He felt the telltale split, the first sign that Kirit was losing to his lust. Cody grabbed Kirit's arm with one hand and slipped the other under Kirit's tunic, searching for... *Ah, there.* The rough scrape of scales under his fingers sent a little thrill through Cody, one that went straight to his groin. He loved this, arousing Kirit to the point where the dragon began losing control of his forms. Having that kind of power over a man who prided himself on his self-discipline was exhilarating.

"Missed you," Kirit whispered.

Cody laughed. "It was only a day."

"Too long," was the reply, given between kisses. "Never survive two months."

"We'll just have to stock up," Cody said, pressing close until he could feel his dragon from nipples to cock. "I won't risk having you go all scaly for good."

Kirit nuzzled Cody's neck, nipping gently at first, then harder, until Cody could feel the scrape of his sharp canines. He shivered.

"Love that."

"I know."

Kirit sounded smug, but Cody decided to give him a pass this time. The reaction was justified, not that he would ever tell Kirit. Although it was pretty obvious, the way Cody fell apart every time those teeth came into contact with his neck. Or his chest. Or any part of him, really.

"More," he urged around a moan.

"My mate is needing."

"God, yes."

Kirit tugged and pulled, arranging Cody to his liking. Somewhere between lying on top of Kirit and lying on top of the pillows, Cody managed to lose his clothes.

"I still think you're using magic," Cody teased.

Kirit smiled, something that he didn't do very often. They were rare, and usually just for Cody. He loved that even more than the biting.

"I'm eager," Kirit said. "Clothes get in the way."

"I'm still not wandering the caves naked," Cody replied dryly. "It's too damn cold. Bloody reptile."

Kirit smiled again before sitting up and stripping off his tunic. Cody trailed his gaze over the wide expanse of Kirit's chest, the sleek, tanned skin giving way to glittering red and gold scales in patches. It was a strangely natural look, the scales blending with the skin instead of standing out. He reached out to touch, but Kirit slapped his hands away.

"Hey!"

"Patience, mate," Kirit said with a smirk.

Cody was going to complain some more, but then Kirit stood and stripped off his pants. It was a slow process. Kirit favored tight leather pants that molded to his thighs and had to be almost peeled off. Cody wasn't complaining. The process was almost as hot to watch as the end result.

Kirit stood naked in front of Cody and let him look his fill, big feet planted on the stone, legs spread wide. The stance made a fantastic foil for the big balls and hard cock.

Cody swallowed and reached out again. This time, Kirit didn't stop him.

Cody kept his touch light, trailing just the tips of his fingers along the hard surface, tracing the veins that bulged along one side.

Kirit growled, only able to withstand the gentle caress for a few moments before he broke. He dropped down on top of Cody, careful as always to catch his weight on his hands. No matter how aroused Kirit became, he never forgot how much larger he was than Cody.

It was only one of the many reasons why Cody loved him so much.

Another of those reasons was prodding his thigh, hot and insistent. Their mouths met again, hard and rough. Cody clutched at Kirit's shoulders, sucking and licking at the dragon's mouth. Kirit's hips were moving, his erection rubbing against Cody, leaving a wet trail behind. He slid one hand down Cody's chest, pausing briefly to tweak one nipple before moving lower.

He bypassed Cody's groin, and Cody whimpered in protest. The sound cut off abruptly when one of those thick fingers unceremoniously invaded his ass. Cody thrust up, trying to take the digit in farther.

Kirit was grinning again. "Someone has been playing," he said, obviously feeling the slight give to the muscles and the lingering wetness from the lube Cody had used before falling asleep.

"What can I say? I missed you, too."

Cody gasped when Kirit added a second finger, slick with lubricant, and moaned at the third.

"Where the hell do you always get the lube?" Cody said, his voice breathy.

Kirit smiled and did something wicked with his probing fingers. Cody forgot all about magical lube as his world devolved into heat and passion, the scent of lust thick in the air.

"More, more." Curses accompanied the pleas as Cody wiggled and strained, wanting, no, *needing* more than a few fingers.

He got his wish quickly. Kirit was too impatient to tease him for long. The thick head of his cock pressed against Cody's entrance. Cody relaxed, welcoming the pressure and the slight tinge of pain as Kirit entered him, slowly and relentlessly.

"My mate," Kirit said around a growl. "Only mine."

"Only yours, big guy." Cody nipped Kirit on the shoulder, knowing his blunt teeth would barely make an impression.

Kirit got the message, anyway. "Only yours," he added. "Always."

Kirit started out slow, but Cody wasn't having any of it, not today. He wrapped his legs around Kirit's waist and shoved, using a little trick Chaos had taught him a few weeks before. It was supposed to be a self-defense move, but it worked well here, too. Kirit landed on his back, Cody on top of him.

"Mate!"

"Too slow," Cody said in a growl of his own, a pretty damn good one, if he did say so himself. Maybe Chaos was right and the dragons were rubbing off on him. He could think of worse things.

"No thinking of others when I'm inside you," Kirit demanded.

Cody rolled his eyes then gave Kirit another long kiss. It worked, distracting the big guy from his momentary flare of possessiveness.

"Love you," Cody assured his dragon.

Kirit emitted a low roar, the sound rife with satisfaction.

Dragons.

Cody squeezed his inner muscles, clamping down tightly on Kirit's cock. The action had the desired effect. Kirit's eyes quite literally rolled back in his head as he howled in pleasure.

Cody rubbed his hands along the massive pectoral muscles underneath him, now completely covered in warm, scratchy scales.

"Just lie back and enjoy the ride," he said with a wicked grin.

He started to move, rising up until just the tip of Kirit's cock was still inside him. Then he dropped back down, letting gravity do most of the work. Kirit roared again, this time loudly. It made Cody's ears ring, and his grin widened.

He got a good rhythm going, nice and irregular to drive Kirit nuts. He went up and down, rocked from side to side, even did that little circular thing that Kirit loved so much. He soon had his dragon bellowing. Smoke was filling the air again, but this time it was most decidedly not from anger.

Sweat dripped down Cody's body, and he was panting from a combination of exertion and arousal.

"Need more, Kirit, please."

Kirit grunted, but complied, and there it was. The biggest reason Cody loved this position—aside from the fact that it put him in control of his big dragon. Kirit latched onto his hip with one big hand to hold him steady and used the other to cup his balls. The heat from Kirit's large palm soaked into his skin. Calloused fingers closed around his penis and began stroking roughly. The sensation was almost too much, too hard, but Cody was too far gone to complain. The hard touch, the heat, and the way Kirit's cock kept brushing against his prostate...

Gods, almost...there...

Kirit grunted, his climax hitting hard and fast. He arched up into Cody, freezing in position. His hand stopped moving while he rode out the waves of pleasure.

Cody tossed his head back, feeling the searing heat bathe his insides. He groaned and shifted until the pulsing head hit just the right spot. Kirit squeezed, and it was all over.

Cody shouted, spurting cum all over Kirit. The pleasure dragged on until it was almost painful.

"Enough," he gasped.

Kirit immediately let go of Cody's cock and wrapped his arms around Cody's waist. The last spurt dribbled from him as his orgasm slowly subsided. Drained, Cody dropped forward, thankful that his dragon was strong enough to take his weight.

"Damn, big guy," he said hoarsely.

"Indeed."

"One of these days, that's going to kill me."

Kirit dropped a kiss on top of Cody's head. "No, no leaving me, mate. I'm yours. No one else can have me."

"No one else would want you," Cody teased.

He got a swift smack on the arse for his cheek. Cody wiggled.

"Oooh, do that again."

Kirit started to laugh. "Ah, mate. When I can breathe again. Perhaps after a nap."

"You dragons and your naps."

Cody snuggled closer, though. Now that he thought about it, a nap did sound like a great idea. Or rather, going back to sleep, because the sun still hadn't come up.

"Sleep," Kirit urged, halfway there himself.

Cody patted his big dragon, then let himself relax. He could feel drying cum on his skin. They were going to get stuck together again, but he couldn't muster the energy to move.

He listened to the sound of his dragon, breath deepening until a soft snore filled the room. Cody smiled, but the expression quickly faded.

My dragon. What the hell am I going to do without you for two goddamn months?

Cody curled closer and let sleep creep in, not wanting to think about it. Ever. His last thought before he slipped into slumber was, *I'm going to give Seamus a swift kick in the arse when I see him next time.*

Maybe the king wasn't to blame, but he certainly made a nice target for Cody's ire.

Chapter Four

A scream rent the pre-dawn stillness. Nyx sent the poor woman a mental apology and twisted his big body, ducking below the tree line. No sense in causing a full-scale panic. He had thought it was still dark enough to keep him hidden. Now that he looked, though, the tips of his dark wings were gilded gold with the rising sun.

Time to come back to Earth.

Nyx dodged branches, looking for a clear spot. The closest he found was occupied by a large herd of nice, fat sheep. Nyx thought about snagging some breakfast, but Raven got cranky when they stole livestock. It tended to stir up the locals into a minor frenzy. It was tempting, though.

What could Nyx say? He was extremely fond of mutton.

Nyx folded his wings and dropped heavily to the ground. A deep exhalation, and the world grew in size as he shrank. Nyx stretched his arms over his head, working some of the kinks out of his back. *Goddess, I needed that.*

He hadn't slept much. Or, if he were honest, at all. Bad dreams had haunted his rest and had finally driven him out of the inn and into the sky at some no doubt ridiculous hour. He didn't remember details of his nightmares, just blood and pain and terrified mismatched eyes. He had hoped the flight would relax him, but Nyx still couldn't shake the sense of foreboding.

Was he doing the right thing? He really wished he had an answer.

It would help if Nyx could discuss the whole damn mate thing with someone, anyone. But even if he wanted to take the time, he wasn't sure who to talk to. Any of the dragons would tell him to leap in and not look back. Seamus would lecture about the sanctity of mating. And Cody would probably smack Nyx and tell him he was being an idiot. None of them would understand the doubts battering at Nyx's self-confidence.

I'm not good enough for my little mate, and I know it.

If it were only that, Nyx could work his way through the problems. It was more, though. Mixed in with his nightmares had been Cody, faced bruised and battered from the attack he had suffered shortly after arriving at the palace.

Very well, so in reality it had only been a black eye, and Cody had later beaten his attacker into the ground. But if Cody, who was strong, independent and tough, could be hurt, what chance did Nyx have of protecting Pol? Pol was tiny and delicate, and would probably bruise if someone sneezed too hard in his direction. The Fae court could be dangerous—deadly, even—and Nyx couldn't stop obsessing.

Pol was just so damn small. Even thinking about sex made Nyx cringe. He wanted Pol, desperately, but how could they make love without Nyx hurting him? Nyx wasn't as big as some of his fellow dragons, but he was still larger than most humans. Hell, his cock was probably the size of the Pixie's damn arm. He would split the little guy in two before he even made it all the way inside Pol's arse.

The logistics simply don't work.

And yet, he couldn't bring himself to turn away. Pol was *his* mate, and he wanted to grab onto the Pixie and never let go.

He had never been so confused in his life — and he didn't like it. Not one bit.

Nyx grumbled to himself as he hopped a nearby fence, leaving the sheep behind. One gave a startled bleep and they all scattered. *Stupid things… Now they run. They didn't even notice when they had a dragon in their midst. No wonder they're so easy to catch.*

He craved more challenging prey. It was a dragon thing, as Cody would say. They tended to work through emotions in a rather violent manner. What he wouldn't give to pound on Chaos for a while. The youngest dragon made a great relief for any and all frustrations.

Unfortunately, Chaos was with the other dragons, back at the palace, leaving Nyx with the same problem as before. No one to talk to, and no one to fight with.

Emotions were horrible things.

Nyx strode across the darkened countryside, shivering a little in the early morning chill. Stupid, to be out here freezing when he could have stayed inside the nice, warm inn.

Oh, well. Nyx knew he wasn't really known for his intelligence, and he occasionally had an impulse-control issue. He needed to take his mate and go home before he got into any more trouble.

Nyx didn't do so well on his own. He needed the support and advice of his clutch. Trying to make such life-altering decisions on his own was making his gut ache.

And who knows? Maybe Pol will have decided he doesn't want a dragon, after all, and the whole thing will go away.

Somehow, that thought didn't make him feel any better.

* * * *

Pol settled onto the bench, propping his bag against the trunk of a nearby tree. He leaned back, looking at the stars overhead. The birds were beginning to awaken, their songs replacing that of the crickets and frogs that made the garden their home. The sky was lightening, dawn coming quickly. He wanted to reach up and shove it back, keep the cover of night for just a few more hours. It wasn't just because his life would soon be changing. He liked the night, liked the sounds and smells, the way the dark wrapped him close and hid him from view.

Pol would miss this garden. He knew it as well as he knew his tiny room on the third floor of the building barely visible through the sheltering trees. Better, perhaps. He certainly spent more time here. It was the Pixie in him—he couldn't resist the lure of nature, not for very long.

Off to the left, a nightingale began chirping and trilling. The sound made him smile. Pol opened his mouth instinctively, ready to sing along. Then the wind shifted ever so slightly, bringing with it the scent of the sea. He pressed his lips together, suppressing the sound.

Can't sing here. It's too close to the ocean.

It was a constant struggle, one he had to wage daily, to suppress the music. That was the downside of his garden. The Red Curtain sat at the north edge of town, and the coastline was only a few miles away. Far enough for sound to carry, at least to *them*.

Pol had avoided discovery for too long to be careless now — not with so much to look forward to.

It was a part of moving inland that thrilled him the most. While he would have said yes to Nyx regardless, the lure of being away from the ocean was almost irresistible. His mother had needed the proximity to the sea. Pol didn't and it was, in fact, growing increasingly dangerous for him to be this close. His mother's people were resourceful. They would eventually find him if he stayed in Parmouth. His father's people had banished Pol — his mother's would kill him. While his parents were alive, it hadn't been an issue. No one wanted to confront the Duke. On his own, though...

But you're not on your own anymore, are you? No, he had a big, strong dragon now. The thought sent shivers up his spine, the good kind. The ones that led to sensations he really wanted to experience.

A virgin in a brothel. Oh, the irony.

The telltale clank of the side gate opening broke through his thoughts. Pol stood, looking anxiously down the path. He felt the brush of leaves from the flowering plant at his side. Pol gave it a reassuring pat and took a few steps away from the bench.

Two men came into view, one small and one large. Or rather, one large and one comparatively small, because Pol had never considered Raul to be all that short. Next to a dragon, however, he looked tiny. Nyx's size should have made Pol feel childlike, but it didn't. Standing next to Nyx last night he had felt safe. Cherished.

Nyx's broad form barely fit onto the narrow path, and he had to duck branches as he walked. A dark cloak covered him, the hood pulled up to hide the gleam of his hair in the emerging sunlight.

Stop drooling, idiot. Pol wiped his sweaty palms on his over-robe and offered a shaky smile.

The smile he got in return was blinding. Pol found his expression relaxing, becoming more natural and less forced.

Yes, this was the right decision.

He picked up his bag and went forward to face his future.

Nyx knew he looked outwardly impassive, but inside he was an absolute mess. His stomach hurt and his jaw ached. He forced himself to unclench his teeth. He couldn't remember ever being this nervous—or feeling quite so awkward. He glanced around and spotted the baggage at Pol's feet, one valise and a larger set of saddle bags. Nyx noted their battered nature and wondered if Pol had borrowed them, or if he had done a lot of traveling in his short life. Nyx stepped forward and picked up the saddle bags.

"Is this all you have?" he asked softly.

Pol nodded. "Clothes, mostly, and a few mementos. I wasn't allowed... I had to leave a lot behind when my parents died."

"I'm sorry," Nyx said, but he bit his tongue on further questions after noticing the servant still hovering a few feet away. There was a story there. It didn't escape Nyx's attention, what Pol had started to say. They would have plenty of time to discuss their mutual pasts, however, away from any eager listeners.

Nyx switched the bag to one hand and reached out with other, pleased beyond words when Pol placed his hand in Nyx's. Nyx gave it a squeeze, although the size difference gave him the shivers—and not the good kind. *How in the name of the gods am I supposed to — nope, not thinking about this right now.* The last thing Nyx needed was to try to climb on a horse while sporting a rampant erection. Uncomfortable, to say the least.

"Come, then, *mellitus*," Nyx said. "It is a long journey."

* * * *

It typically took two days by horse to travel from Parmouth to Aleusia. Of course, Nyx was used to traveling with scouts, couriers or small military escorts. They moved quite a bit faster than your average civilian.

In this case, their journey looked to be stretching out indefinitely. He and Pol had left the previous morning, the sun was setting on their second day, and they were only halfway to Aleusia.

That was fine by Nyx. He wasn't in any hurry to return. There were, as far as he knew, no pressing issues awaiting his attention. And he wasn't ready to take Pol back to the palace. He didn't want the questions, didn't want to deal with...anything. If he didn't have to explain Pol's past, then he didn't have to think about it.

It was childish and selfish, he knew that, but he couldn't seem to help it.

There was another reason, too, one that was still selfish but at least more reasonable. Nyx had watched the hell Cody and Kirit had gone through, and he wanted to keep Pol to himself. Just for a while, until they got to know each other better. His little Pixie didn't need to be thrown into the viper's nest that the court could often be, not without feeling secure in his place as a dragon's consort.

A few weeks. Then Nyx would figure out something else. Besides, he doubted he could keep Pol's presence a secret from Seamus any longer than that. The king was a nosey bastard.

Nyx dropped his pack on the bed and surveyed the small room he had rented for the night. He resisted the urge to wrinkle his nose. It wasn't bad, but it was a far cry from the comforts of the palace. It was, however, worlds better than sleeping on the ground, which they had done the night before. Pol hadn't complained, but he hadn't been happy, either. Nyx had found that he had the typical dragon compulsion to coddle his mate. He had begun looking for a decent inn hours before sunset.

Pol stepped through the door behind Nyx, examining the room with wide, curious eyes.

Damn, he is so cute. The thought struck Nyx every time he looked at his Pixie.

Pol suddenly gave a running leap, landing on the bed. The ancient mattress groaned loudly in protest and Nyx cringed, waiting for the whole thing to collapse. Miraculously, it didn't.

"Bed," Pol declared, spreading his arms wide. Then he sat up, scowling. "I think it has more lumps than the ground."

"I'm sorry," Nyx said. "At least they're soft lumps."

Pol jabbed with his finger at a spot on the mattress. "I don't know. This one is pokey."

"Pokey?" Just like that, the tension burst with an almost audible pop. Nyx started to laugh. It only took a moment for Pol to join him.

And then Pol stopped laughing and started looking sexy. Nyx swallowed.

"Come join me." The Pixie patted beside him in invitation.

Nyx's feet moved, seemingly of their own accord, and he found himself getting closer and closer to the bed.

Then he was there, sinking down on the mattress.

"Damn, you weren't kidding about this bed." Nyx grumbled wordlessly, giving an experimental bounce. Something...*pokey*...hit him in the arse, and it was, indeed, harder than the rock he'd slept on the night before.

"I don't think we'll get much sleep on this," Nyx said.

"Hmmm. We'll have to come up with something else to keep us occupied, then, won't we?"

"Damn."

"Am I making you uncomfortable?" Pol asked with maddening innocence, sliding ever closer.

"Umm...no, of course...not... I... What are you doing?"

"Do you really need to ask?" The words were damn near purred as Pol wrapped his arms around Nyx's neck.

"Oh, damn," Nyx said again, just before Pol initiated a kiss potent enough to make his toes curl.

Pol couldn't believe he was acting like this. He wasn't a bold person, not in the slightest. But something about Nyx make him ache, made him need, in a way that completely demolished his normal inhibitions.

He needed to be closer, to crawl inside Nyx until they merged into one being. Pol settled for climbing into the dragon's lap, straddling his thighs and pressing their chests together. He tilted his head, nipping at the corner of Nyx's mouth. He ran his tongue along the dry, cracked skin of his lips, soothing the tiny stings.

"Mate," he whispered.

"Yes," Nyx whispered back.

Pol pushed, shocked when Nyx actually tumbled backwards. The dragon grunted as his back hit the not-so-soft surface beneath them.

"Sorry," Pol said.

Nyx didn't answer, too busy exploring with hands and mouth. Pol arched his back as Nyx ran his large hands up Pol's spine.

Someone pounded on the door.

Pol yelped and tumbled sideways, sliding off his large, comfy dragon.

"What the hell do you want?" Nyx bellowed. His eyes were glowing, and tiny puffs of smoke had started to appear around his nostrils.

"Shh," Pol said. "Let's not set the room on fire, okay?"

Nyx muttered something and stood, crossing the room in two big strides. He yanked open the door.

"What?" he snarled again.

"S-s-sorry," a voice filled with terror stammered. "A m-m-message."

A piece of paper was thrust into the room, then the man fled, damn near running, from the sound of it.

"Goddamn wizards," Nyx said. He ripped open the envelope, scanning the contents. "All that magic at their fingertips, and they send me a damned letter. If they can track me anywhere in Faerie, why the hell can't they figure out a more efficient communication method?"

Pol figured it would be prudent to keep his mouth shut. Nyx didn't seem in the mood to appreciate having rhetorical questions answered.

Nyx sighed a moment later. "I'm sorry, *mellitus*. I have been summoned. We are going to have to take the fast way home."

"The fast way?"

Pol wasn't sure he liked the sound of that.

Nyx began sorting through their luggage, talking under his breath to himself. "Put everything you need in that one," he said, gesturing toward the bag with straps. "I'll have the rest sent by land."

"By land?"

Nyx consolidated their luggage into two bags and disappeared out of the door, saying something about arrangements. He came back moments later with a scowl and a large amount of rope.

Pol decided it would be better not to ask.

He soon found himself jogging down the hall after Nyx, their bags banging against his leg as he hurried to keep up.

"Nyx?" He panted for breath as he juggled one of Nyx's packs, trying to get a better grip.

"Sorry." Nyx took the bag before he could drop it, but then moved even faster toward the front entrance.

"Apologies," he called to the inn owner. The man looked up from behind the long bar on one side of the front room. "We won't be staying. Keep the payment anyway. Is there an empty field nearby?"

Field?

The inn owner seemed equally confused, but answered, "Just on the other side of town, there's a side path leading into the trees."

"Thank you."

Pol added his own thanks and kept moving. He followed Nyx out of the front door and down the dusty street.

"What about the horses?"

"I am bloody well not taking the horses," Nyx said. "That would be ridiculous."

"Ridicul—never mind."

Talking and running took too much effort, so Pol resolved to play one of his favorite games, 'wait and see'. He had found that you spent far less time looking like an idiot if you simply practiced a little patience.

In this case, his patience wasn't necessarily rewarded. They took the small path, through the trees and into a large open pasture, and he still didn't know why they were there.

"Nyx—"

"Stand back," Nyx ordered. "And don't move."

Pol scowled. He dropped their luggage, folded his arms across his chest, and waited. "Thought I was going to *finally* lose my virginity, but what am I doing? Standing like an idiot in an empty field waiting for— Holy Mother of All!"

Pol knew his face had likely gone stark white, and his legs had suddenly developed a bad tremble and a dislike of keeping him upright. He stared with eyes so wide they ached as the magic rushed over him, leaving behind something he had only seen in books.

Dragon.

Dark scales gleamed in the sunlight, glinting in painful flashes. They ranged from a deep, dark brownish-red at the chest to pure, stark black on the back. The massive, blocky head swiveled to fix him in the penetrating stare of one green eye. A very familiar green.

"Wow." Pol really wasn't sure what else you said when your lover turned into a creature of myth right in front of you. Well, potential lover, anyway. "Those spikes look really dangerous."

A dull matte black, they marched in a straight line along his spine, from the join of the dragon's shoulders clear to the tip of its swishing tail. Each one was probably the length of Pol's arm, and at least as thick.

The Nyx-Dragon rumbled, a puff of smoke erupting around his head. It moved closer, reaching out with its front claws. It plucked the bags Pol was guarding off the ground in a move that was almost comically delicate. The dragon grunted, contorting itself and jerking its head significantly at its back.

"Oh, no." Pol started to back up. "No. Absolutely not."

The dragon grunted again and more smoke filled the clearing.

Pol had a dawning suspicion about 'the fast way', and he wasn't at all happy about it.

The dragon opened its mouth wide, revealing row after row of razor sharp teeth, and roared. The force of the sound nearly knocked Pol off his feet.

"Stop that," he yelled. "Fine. But don't you dare drop me!"

Pol took a deep breath. *Well, Pol, you wanted an adventure, didn't you? I think this certainly qualifies.*

With a large sigh, the dragon folded its legs and dropped to the ground, sending Pol staggering again when the impact caused a mini-earthquake.

Pol narrowed his eyes at the creature, not sure if he wanted to run from it or hit it. "So childish," he muttered.

And really, he was just trying to distract himself from the fact that he was about to *mount a dragon.*

The dragon blew more smoke in impatience, and Pol coughed as the stench of ash and brimstone tickled his throat and nostrils.

"Stop that," he demanded again. "You're making it hard to see."

When the air cleared a little, Pol took several hesitant steps. He finally drew close to the dragon, amazed at its sheer mass and the amount of heat it emanated.

"Just don't...don't eat me, okay?"

The dragon turned its head again, stared at Pol, then...*rolled its eyes?*

"Maybe you are still in there," Pol said. "Nyx?"

The dragon bared its teeth and, after a period of sheer and utter panic, Pol decided it was giving him the dragon version of a smile.

"Don't scare me like that. I don't know much about shape-shifting creatures, all right? I don't know how much of you sticks around when you're all scaly."

Then he was standing right next to the dragon, reaching out to touch the shining scales.

"Oh, they're soft," Pol declared in surprise. He had thought they would be hard, like maille, but they weren't. It was more like touching flesh than armor. They were warm, giving slightly under his touch.

The Nyx-Dragon grumbled some more, the sound growing ever more impatient.

"Okay," Pol said, more to himself than the dragon. "Okay, I'm coming."

He reached up as far as he could, until his fingers brushed the hard, slick surface of one of the dragon's spikes. He gripped it tightly, using it to haul himself up into the air. Way up.

Pol tried very hard not to look down, because from here, the fall would probably hurt. Especially if Nyx stepped on him with one of those big feet. If he landed within range of the nasty claws on the ends of those big feet, well, Nyx might find himself without a mate before they even made it to bed.

And that would be a huge shame.

I can't die. I haven't had sex yet.

With that bracing thought, Pol managed to finish hauling himself up into the air. The dragon moved underneath him and Pol screamed, scrabbling wildly for a secure hand-hold.

The dragon huffed, its sides moving, and Pol realized it was laughing at him.

Before Pol could think better of it, he reached up and whacked the dragon on the top of its big head.

Oh, shit, he thought, immediately regretting it. Instead of getting angry, though, the dragon looked...chastised?

"That's better," Pol said with a nod.

The dragon moved again. One long claw was offered, a bag dangling from it.

"What am I supposed to do with that?" Pol asked.

The dragon shoved the bag at him again. With a huff of his own, Pol took it, hanging it from a nearby spike.

"I guess these things are useful, after all," Pol said. "At least now I know what the rope is for."

After securing their bags, he quickly found another use for the spikes. He used one as a backrest and wrapped his arms around another, settling himself into position in roughly the center point between the wing joints. It was surprisingly comfortable and, even better, seemed quite secure. Especially once he used the last of the rope to tie himself in place—he wasn't taking a chance of falling off.

Without any warning, the big body heaved, the wings flapped, and they were launched into the air in blatant defiance of every law of science Pol had ever studied.

He wasn't ashamed to admit it. He screamed like a little girl.

In seconds, they were far, far above the ground. Pol didn't even want to think how far. The wind whipped his hair into a frenzy, and he made a mental note. *Next time you go flying, put the hair in a braid.*

Once Pol's heart had stopped pounding loudly in his ears and once he'd decided he wasn't going to go tumbling to his doom, he began to relax. Then he began to enjoy it. The world was quiet, just the wind and the flap of wings. He leaned against the spike at his back, breathing deeply. The air was crisp and smelled...pure. Bright, if something could smell bright. Pol couldn't help it and started humming under his breath.

Nyx gave a small screech, the sound reminiscent of the honk of a swan, strangely enough. Pol didn't know dragons could emit noises like that, and it made him giggle. He leaned to the side, watching the clouds drift below. He saw the occasional flash of green from the breaks in the clouds, then they moved beyond them all together.

The view was nothing short of magnificent. Pol had never seen anything like it. He lay flat, hugging his dragon's neck, and watched the world pass by. Valleys and fields, rivers and lakes. Shadows shaded the mountains in the distance, its peaks wreathed in dark clouds. Lightning flashed within, a mesmerizing display of light and dark.

"Thank you," he whispered to Nyx, knowing the dragon probably couldn't hear him, but needing to say the words anyway.

Then he began to sing.

Chapter Five

Nyx couldn't get that damn song out of his head. Not the melody, but the essence of it. Haunting, powerful...magical. Incredibly magical. It had been beautiful. He could have listened to his mate sing all day. But the memory was making him twitchy.

Nyx shoved open the wooden door, the hinges protesting with a loud groan. He was growing very tired of inns. At least this one was a step up from the last establishment. The bed didn't look all that comfortable, but at least it appeared free of lumps.

He sighed and stretched his arms over his head, cracking the bones in his spine. Changing forms often left him stiff and sore. It could take hours for the effects to wear off and the world to settle. In the meantime, everything felt strange, the wrong size, and his senses never seemed to work properly.

Pol looked around their room at the inn in confusion. "This is where you live?"

Nyx tried to smile as he closed the door. "No, this is just temporary. I have rooms at the palace, but we won't have any privacy there. I'll make other arrangements tomorrow."

Nyx needed to find somewhere to stash his mate. Stash. That sounded wrong. Like he was ashamed of Pol. And he wasn't, not at all. But he wasn't ready to share, and now there were more pressing issues to worry about, anyway. Namely, that song of Pol's.

"All right." Pol was looking at him suspiciously, but didn't push, for which Nyx was extremely grateful. He was feeling guilty enough for his behavior. Having to explain it would only make him feel like an absolute bastard.

"Come here," Nyx said softly, opening up his arms. He was thrilled when Pol walked right into them. Pol wrapped his skinny arms around Nyx's waist and let himself be held. Nyx's low, rumbling purr sounded loud in the quiet room.

"I like that noise," Pol said.

"You liked flying, too."

Pol tipped his head back, his smile wide. "I did. It was marvelous."

"I'm glad. Cody, the other dragon-mate, hates it."

"Mmmm. He's missing out."

"I always thought so."

"It made me happy, seeing the world from a new perspective. So big and beautiful."

"And when you're happy, you sing?" Damn it, he hadn't been going to ask. If he didn't ask, he didn't know, and if he didn't know, then he didn't have to deal with it. Because he could see the problems looming, large and terrifying, and he just wanted to bask, damn it.

"I do. It's a thing."

"A Pixie thing?"

"No. My...other half." Pol was clearly reluctant to divulge the nature of that other half. Not a good sign.

"Ah. Other half. Of course. It was...quite lovely." *Damn it. What species has a thing for singing?* Several came to mind, but none of them boded well. Pixie genetics tended to stack weirdly with other powerful species. Too much power, and Seamus took notice. Not in a good way, either.

"You're angry." Pol looked ready to burst into tears, those pretty eyes all red and watery. "I knew it! Nobody wants a stupid half-breed."

"Hush, *mellitus*," Nyx interrupted. "I think you're marvelous." He let go of his mate and began to pace.

"Nyx?"

"Sorry. I knew you weren't pure Pixie. It's not a problem."

"No, you just like to curse and pace. Don't lie."

So his little mate had some spunk to him, after all. It made Nyx smile, until his mind dropped back into its earlier thought pattern. Nyx started to pace again.

"Would you hold still?" Pol reached out when Nyx passed and grabbed his arm, pulling him to a stop. "You're making me dizzy."

"S—"

"If you say sorry again, I'm going to hit you. Stop apologizing and talk to me." Pol sighed. "Are all dragons this annoying?"

"I'm told so, yes."

Pol squinted, the skin around his pretty eyes crinkling, then he laughed. "You look cute when you brood."

"Dragons do not brood," Nyx declared indignantly.

"Oh, but they do."

That impish grin had him aching in an instant.

"You take that back," Nyx said with a grin of his own.

"Nope." With another smirk, Pol took off running. It was a small room—he couldn't get far. Nyx caught him in a few strides, tackling him, albeit carefully. They landed on the large rug in front of the fireplace.

"Now that you've caught me, what are you going to do with me?" Pol asked from his position pinned underneath Nyx.

In answer, Nyx kissed him. He meant it to be quick. He needed to get to the palace and find out why Seamus had called him back. But he quickly lost control and the short kiss turned into a long, drawn-out affair. He couldn't seem to make himself let go of those soft lips or untangle his hands from the silky, tangled mass of dark blue hair. Pol wrapped himself around Nyx like a barnacle, legs and arms pulling their bodies close. Pol's tongue tangled with Nyx's, teasing and tasting. He gave a small squeak of delight as he explored along the sharp fangs, then discovered the tiny slit in Nyx's tongue. Nyx hissed, the sound more reptile than human.

Gods, but his mate tasted sweet, like a crisp apple, complete with the scent and feel of autumn. He tilted his head, slanting his lips across Pol's, deepening the connection. He could quite happily spend all day kissing his mate.

Or he could, if there weren't other parts of his body clamoring for attention. His leather pants were becoming painfully constricting, and Nyx could feel an answering hardness pressing against him.

"Mate," his little Pixie whispered. "I need. What do I need? I don't... Oh, do that again."

Nyx gladly obliged, thrusting his hips and providing them both with a delightful sense of friction.

"Skin. This is so much better with skin," Nyx gasped. But he didn't want to let go long enough to strip, and Pol was moving so sinuously, and…

Pol gasped, body going stiff, and shook heavily in Nyx's arms. Nyx groaned as the smell of Pol's release filled the air, tangy and pungent.

"You… Did you just… Gods above, that's incredible." And incredibly flattering, too, that he could make his little mate come with just a kiss and a little rubbing. He reached down, cupping Pol's softening cock, feeling the dampness of the cloth under his touch.

"Incredible," he whispered again.

"Oh. Oh, I liked that. I did. Can I…? What about you?" Pol wiggled, and Nyx groaned again, this time the sound a little pained.

"Keep that up," he said, "and I'll be a very happy dragon."

Pol followed instructions, grinding his slender body against Nyx. Then he wiggled some more, reaching down to touch Nyx's groin with one hand.

"Oh, gods."

Nyx tossed his head back, loving the feel of his mate's small hand touching him so carefully. Pol kept up the tentative, light caresses, and it was enough to drive Nyx mad.

"Harder, *carissime*," he ordered in a hoarse, nearly indecipherable voice. "You can touch me harder."

He nearly cried when, instead of doing that, Pol removed his hand entirely. Those same small hands pushed at his shoulders, until Nyx rolled onto his back. The rug didn't offer much padding, and something was digging into his spine, but Nyx couldn't bring himself to care. Not with Pol starting at him, eyes bright with desire.

Pol began working at the fastenings to Nyx's pants, and it was enough to make Nyx's eyes roll back in his head. Pol's teasing touch as he brushed his fingers against Nyx's painfully erect cock was driving him mad.

"*Carissime*, I need more. Please."

It seemed to take an eternity, but Pol finally freed Nyx's erection, and the first touch of skin on skin was nearly enough to make Nyx explode. He gasped, words fleeing into the blackness of pure sensation. Pol's touch was hesitant at first, but his little mate quickly gained confidence, stroking him from root to tip. He caressed the head of Nyx's cock with one hand, the other grasping the base. His small hand couldn't encircle Nyx's cock completely, but Pol certainly tried his best. The touches became faster, keeping time with Nyx's increasing breath.

Nyx could feel his climax creeping up, tightening his balls and zipping along his nerves, his entire body going taut.

Pol repeated the move, massaging that one spot right behind Nyx's sac that made him see stars. A few more strokes, and the crest of pleasure broke into waves of sensation. Nyx couldn't even yell, every centimeter of his body consumed by the force of his release. He stared through hazy vision at his mate, watching in wonder as Pol raised one hand, licking cum from his fingers. It sent another burst through Nyx, and he gasped through a second climax. It was damn near painful.

Finally, after an endless age, his muscles began to relax in that post-orgasmic bliss that he loved so much. He raised one hand, brushing his mate's pale cheek, then tucking some loose strands behind one pointed ear.

"Did I do it right?" Pol was chewing nervously on his lip, eyes anxious.

Nyx would have laughed if he'd had the energy. "Hell, yes," he said in a rasping voice. "Any better and I think you would have killed me."

Pol laughed, cuddling close, not seeming to care in the slightest that he was getting his clothing covered in cum and sweat, which was when Nyx realized that his little mate was still fully dressed, while Nyx himself lay on the rug with his pants open, his spent cock hanging out.

"Gods, the indignity," he said wryly.

"I won't tell," his mate promised, mischief in his smile. "So long as we can do that again."

"You're damn right we'll do it again," Nyx promised. *And again, and again.*

Oh, yes, Nyx completely understood Kirit's obsession with his mate now. He was rapidly heading in the same direction.

"Again," he said, pulling Pol close for a kiss.

Chapter Six

Pol stared at the ceiling, dreamily replaying that night in front of the fire. Nyx's hands and mouth and…

He sighed, sitting up and running his hands through his unbound hair. There were tangles, and he worked them loose with his fingers.

That night had been two days ago, and ever since, Pol had been cooped up in this stupid room with nothing to do. He had tried to help downstairs, but the appalled looks had sent him scurrying away. Then he had tried spending time in the stables. He liked horses, and it at least got him outdoors. But the stares of the grooms had made his spine itch, and once again, he'd been forced to retreat.

Nyx was busy doing whatever it was dragons did with their time. Pol saw him at random intervals and, if he was lucky, he received a kiss before Nyx left again. Nyx was always apologetic and promised over and over that he was making arrangements, but in the meantime, Pol was left…how did the humans put it? Twiddling his thumbs?

He wasn't used to being idle. There had always been more chores than time at The Red Curtain. Before that, there had been studies or working in his garden, or lessons. Gods above, so many lessons—comportment, customs, diplomacy, geography.

He hadn't been sorry to give up that part of his old life.

Pol worked the last of the tangles loose then flopped back down on the bed. He went back to counting the braces in the ceiling—twelve—then finding the cracks.

The sound of a key in the lock made him sit up again, heart thumping in excitement. Nyx entered a moment later, and Pol smiled.

"Hi," he said.

"Hi," Nyx said with a smile of his own.

Pol watched his mate, chewing on his bottom lip. It was ridiculous, but he still felt shy and awkward around the big, confident dragon. A few days hadn't been enough time to change that.

To his surprise, Nyx paused just inside the door, looking equal parts excited and anxious. "I have something to show you."

Pol popped off the bed like a rabbit out of a bush. He was going somewhere!

He found his shoes halfway under the bed and his outer robe was draped over one of the chairs in front of the tiny table. He pulled it on, closing the fastenings.

"All ready," he declared.

Nyx smiled, the expression deepening the lines around his eyes, and held out his hand. Pol took it eagerly.

There was a distinct chill to the air, but Pol didn't care. He looked around with wide eyes as they walked, taking in the sights and smells. It was all so very different from Parmouth. Colder, the colors less vivid, and yet it had a charm that was undeniable. The clatter of hooves and wheels was loud on the cobbled roads as they passed through the business district, brick and stone slowly giving way to wood and marble. The architecture was unusual, a strange mix of practical and fanciful. Most of the houses were set up and back from the street, with stairs going up to the front doors and down to the servant's areas.

This wasn't a wealthy area. The homes were small and cozy, many of them showing signs of aging. Thick trees sheltered the walk, though, and flowering bushes were everywhere.

They walked for several blocks before coming to a stop at the intersection of two quiet, narrow streets. The stairs leading to the pale cream door were cracked and the light blue paint on the façade faded to nearly white, but Pol loved the little house on sight.

"It's ours," Nyx said nervously. "I signed the deed earlier today."

"It's darling," Pol exclaimed happily. "Show me the inside?"

There was the smell of must in the air and the furnishings were worn, but the house itself felt warm and welcoming. Pol could feel the happiness in the walls. Happiness and a healthy dose of satisfaction, which made him giggle, because it felt a lot like Nyx did after he came.

"You can change anything you want," Nyx said. He hovered anxiously while Pol explored. "I want you to be comfortable here."

"Oh, I will." Pol smiled. "It's a happy place."

"Happy?"

"Can't you feel it?" Pol spun in a circle in the middle of the small foyer. "So happy."

"If you say so." Nyx's smile was indulgent. "Oh! I haven't shown you the best part yet."

Nyx grabbed Pol's hand and pulled him farther down the hall. They passed the drawing room and the dining room, ending up in front of a short set of stairs. They went down into the kitchen, but Nyx pushed open a door on the right instead. They stepped outside into the sunshine, and Pol gave a little cry of joy.

"I thought you might like this."

"I love it! It's perfect."

The gardens were overgrown and in desperate need of tending, but someone had clearly put a lot of thought and love into them at one point. He could see a neat arrangement of paths stretching through the shrubbery, even if they were almost hidden at points. The garden was fenced, but the area contained in it was probably larger than the house. He began to walk, trailing his fingers along the leaves and caressing flowers. They sang to him, humming in greeting.

The path he was on led to the center of the garden. He pushed past bushes and wove around trees, careful not to step on any protruding roots.

"It's not much," Nyx admitted when they reached the middle. "I think the last owner must have taken a few things."

That was an understatement. Where Pol had expected a haven, he found a blank, empty circle of stone. It looked like there might have been a statue in the middle at one point, but it was gone, leaving behind a patch of dirt punctuated randomly by shaggy patches of grass.

That was all right. It meant he got to put his own touch to the place.

"I'll make it beautiful," he promised. "A few benches, a flower pot or two. Maybe a fountain. It will be wonderful."

"I imagine so." Nyx wasn't looking at the garden.

Pol blushed, still not used to the way Nyx stared at him with such heat and want. And longing. Damn, but the longing made Pol ache, and not always in a good way.

Doesn't Nyx know I'm his for the taking?

He decided to remind the dragon. Pol reached up, tugging until Nyx bent down enough for a kiss.

"Thank you," Pol whispered, brushing their lips together with light touches.

"You're very welcome." Nyx's eyes sparkled, his pleasure evident.

"We should explore some more," Pol declared. "Maybe test out some of the furniture."

There, he should be able to figure that one out.

"I could be persuaded." Nyx kissed him one more time, then pulled away. Pol was glad to see the reluctance in the action, even while he wanted to yank Nyx back.

"We should check upstairs. See if it's furnished."

"You do have good ideas."

Nyx hooked their arms together—it was a bit of an awkward reach—and led the way back indoors. Pol leaned his weight against Nyx's side as they strolled through the greenery.

"Make a list," Nyx said, stroking Pol's side through the many layers of fabric. "Anything you want, hmm? I want you to be happy here."

"I will be," Pol promised. "I could be happy in a cave if you were there, and this is far from a cave."

Wait, why did that comment make Nyx look guilty? *Oh...dragon. Cave.* Maybe Pol should reassure Nyx, but he couldn't bring his mouth to form the words. It wasn't a secret. Pol liked his comforts. He could live in a cold, damp cave if absolutely necessary, but he would really prefer not to.

"Don't worry," Nyx whispered into Pol's ear. "I don't like caves much, either. I've even already brought part of my hoard here. This is home now."

"Your hoard—oh." They had taken a different route back through the house, ending up in what looked like a sitting room. Or rather, what had been a sitting room. Now, it looked more like the inside of a bank vault. Gold and jewels were piled on every surface and glittering in heaps on the floor. "Isn't this a little unsafe?" Pol had visions of black-masked thieves and chortling villains in flowing capes. He probably read too many sensational novels.

"Dragon's hoard," Nyx reminded him. "No one is stupid enough to steal from a dragon's hoard."

"I don't know. There are a lot of stupid people in this world." Pol could think of at least four offhand who fit the description.

Nyx was still, apparently, not worried. He nuzzled Pol again. "You look so pretty. A treasure surrounded by treasures."

"Thanks. I think." Pol wasn't certain whether he should be pleased or offended. He didn't particularly want to be owned. He kept reminding himself that dragons didn't think like most creatures.

"Mmm-hmm. Prettiest of all treasures." Nyx went from nuzzling to kissing. He moved his hand down, cupping Pol's arse briefly before squeezing. Between the touch and Nyx nibbling on his ear, Pol forgot all about treasures and thieves. His world narrowed to Nyx and the piercing green eyes surveying him with such heat.

Nyx lowered him to a clear spot on the floor. A pile of coins towered over his head precariously. Pol squirmed and yanked a diamond necklace out from under his back.

"Can we try a bed this time?" he teased.

"I want to take you surrounded by my other pretties," Nyx insisted.

"Why don't you grab a few and bring them with us? Then you can have comfort and jewelry."

"I suppose."

Then Nyx was kissing him, and Pol decided the floor would be just fine after all.

Chapter Seven

The warm heat of a sunlit day slowly penetrated Pol's sleepy haze. He hummed to himself and rolled over, hand patting for Nyx. Only empty space greeted his quest.

"Damn." Pol was too tired to muster true annoyance. After all, he had been awake into the wee hours of the morning. The sky had been showing hints of a rising sun by the time Pol, exhausted but extremely satisfied, had collapsed into a heap in the messy bedclothes, after they had finally made their way upstairs. Nyx was very inventive.

Of course, it hadn't escaped Pol's notice that, while Nyx was free with touching and pleasure, they had yet to have actual *sex* sex. Every time Pol tried to get that far, Nyx would distract him with skillful trickery. He wanted to feel his mate inside him, so much.

"I wonder if they make rope strong enough to hold dragons," he muttered into his pillow. "If I pin him down and ride him like a donkey, he won't be able to distract me."

And now Pol had the image of a weird donkey-dragon hybrid in his head and it was just disturbing.

"Time to get up," he announced into the silence of the room. "Before my mind takes any more strange tangents."

Pol dragged himself out of the cocoon of his bedding. They had found yesterday that the house was, in fact, fully furnished. The bed had received a thorough testing, and won approval from all relevant parties. It was, in fact, very comfortable, and it took effort for Pol to get his aching body to part from it.

Pol shuffled across the wood floor, heading for the small water closet to the right. He caught a glimpse of his reflection in the floor length mirror and jerked.

"Great Goddess." Pol tugged futilely, trying to restore some semblance of order to the wild mass masquerading as hair. Was that an actual knot? "No wonder Nyx left early. I probably scared him away."

It would take a thorough washing to fix the snarled strands, so Pol turned away from the mirror.

At some point recently, the washroom had been updated with the latest in plumbing inventions. Twenty minutes later, Pol was slipping into the large claw-footed tub full of steaming water with a satisfied sigh.

Which was, naturally, about the time he realized that he didn't have any toiletries. No soap, no shampoo, no cloths or towels. And as far as he knew, his possessions were still back at the inn.

Groaning, Pol dunked his head under the water and blew bubbles. When air forced him to the surface, his thought process was a little less fuzzy.

"Dragons don't do details," he muttered, rubbing water over his limbs in a sad attempt at cleanliness.

"He's demonstrated that often enough in the last few days."

Good grief, had it really only been a few days? In many ways, Pol felt as if he'd known Nyx forever. In a good way. They fit together, easy and comfortable, with enough spice that the relationship would never get dull.

Deciding he was as clean as he was going to get, Pol heaved himself out of the water, ignoring the cascades that splashed onto the tile. It was only water.

Pol padded back to the bedroom, dripping puddles on the floor as he went. An extra sheet in the wardrobe served as a towel, and his inner robes were still fairly clean, even if the outer one was coated in dust and the hem caked in mud.

There was a note stuck on the nightstand that Pol had overlooked earlier. He picked it up, a smile blossoming.

Mellitus,

I was called to the palace for an early meeting. I should return for the evening meal. In the meantime, I have left funds in the top drawer of the desk in the study. Have fun. Be careful.

Your Mate

Really, Nyx could be quite sweet at times.

Pol mentally began making a list of goals for the day. Number one was retrieving his bags. He also needed to see if there was any food in the kitchen and perhaps a staff. Pol didn't mind doing some of the chores, but really, the house was a little large for him to clean by himself, and he wasn't much of a cook.

Halfway down the staircase, the pain hit him. Pol doubled over, gut churning.

"Oh, hells," he gasped. "Not now."

His stupid body wasn't listening as the pain spread. His ears began to ring. Pol hurried down a few more steps, collapsing once he reached the relative safety of the landing. He braced one hand on the wall, the other on the floor, and prepared to ride out the agony of the changes tearing up his body.

The ringing grew louder, until it sounded like someone was banging a drum right in his ear. Pol panted and groaned as his muscles cramped.

The process seemed to last forever. After what felt like hours, his muscles lost some of their tension and the gnawing in his stomach eased. Pol sat back, leaning his weight against the wall, and concentrated on simply breathing. He had a bad habit of holding his breath when the change came over him, which was ridiculous, he knew. It didn't help and usually only made him lightheaded and his lungs ache. The process was bad enough—he didn't need to add to it.

Even after the pain had faded, it took a while before Pol felt capable of moving. His hands shook badly, nausea riding him hard, and he was slick with sweat. When the shaking subsided enough that he wouldn't fall right back on his arse, Pol used the wall to gain his feet. He held his hands out, ostensibly to check the shaking, but really to see if he had morphed into a mutant again.

"Still skin-colored," he said. "That's a good sign, anyway."

Now for the rest of it.

Pol continued downstairs, certain he had seen a mirror near the front door, all the while praying fervently that he still appeared semi-normal. Or at least, as normal as a Pixie-Siren freak like him could be.

The first glimpse of his reflection had him groaning. He studied his still wet hair, now a riotous mass of flame-orange curls, with distaste.

"It could be worse, but that color is definitely going to take some getting used to." At least the eyes looked the same.

But what about Nyx? How in the name of the continents was he going to explain his sudden transformation?

Of course, Nyx already knew about the half-breed thing, but explaining this aspect of his power would lead to the rest of it, and he wasn't ready to go there. It was bad enough being a shape-changer who couldn't control his power, but add in a Pixie who could control nature with song and people began to get nervous — really, really nervous.

Pol sighed. "Why can't anything ever be easy?"

He rubbed his hands over his cheeks, satisfying himself that everything was as it should be. He wrinkled his nose when his hands came away covered in a fine film of perspiration.

"I need another bath. With soap this time." His list began growing in his mind, thoughts racing faster and faster, until he started to pant again.

"Sugar," he finally declared. "I need sugar first." It would help calm the frantic edge left behind by the unexpected change.

He went in search of paper and a pen so he could start an actual list. And sugar. Lots and lots of sugar.

* * * *

The loud banging woke Pol with a start. He slipped sideways, off the edge of the chair, and landed on the wooden floor. The impact was hard and caught him right on the hip, pulling a yelp from his lips. The sound rang around the room.

He stood, rubbing his no-doubt bruised hipbone, and limped to the entryway as more banging reverberated through the empty house.

"Patience is a virtue," Pol lectured the dust motes floating in the entryway. They didn't answer, too busy drifting through the air to settle on the dusty mosaic slate floor.

Pol pulled open the door as someone pounded on it again.

"Delivery." The skinny man shoved something at Pol. Pol was barely able to recognize his luggage before his arms were full and the inn employee was making a hasty retreat.

"I hope everyone in this town isn't so rude."

Pol kicked the front door closed. He hadn't felt like wandering through town in his dirty clothes to retrieve his belongings—even if he had been able to remember the way. It had been easy enough to find a young man willing to carry a message, and a few notes slipped into the request had guaranteed rapid delivery by the inn staff.

It didn't take long for Pol to take another wash, albeit cursory, and unpack his clothing. He shook the wrinkles out as best as possible, then chose the outfit that showed the least muss from being stuffed into his luggage.

Pol turned from side to side, studying his reflection in the full-length mirror. He smoothed his hands along the deep purple fabric of his robe, pleased with the effect. The over-robe was tight on top, belted around his waist, and fell to mid-thigh in thick folds. The stark white of his pants and tunic offset the deep color nicely, and he loved the way the whole outfit contrasted with his hair. The dark orange locks that fell past his shoulders in a curly mass looked startling against the dark fabric, but in a good way. The shade still caught him off-guard every time he caught a glimpse of his reflection, though.

His mother might have passed her shape-changing ability on to Pol, but unfortunately, he had never been able to control it. His appearance randomly changed on him, earlier this morning being only one example. Sometimes he liked it, and sometimes he ended up hiding in his room for a few days. At least this time it was only the hair — he'd spent one memorable week a brilliant shade of purple. It would be hard to impress Nyx with purple skin. That tended to inspire laughter rather than lust.

Pol tied his hair back, arranging it carefully to hide his extremely pointed ears. The curls actually helped with that. When his hair was straight, the tips of his ears often poked through, despite his best efforts.

Pol examined himself one more time then nodded in satisfaction. He knew the very Westren style of his dress wouldn't blend in here in Aleusia, but he liked the way the clothing fit. The drape of the robe was flattering on his slightly chubby body and hid the overly-generous rounded curves of his ass.

He took a small detour to the study to fill the small bag hanging from his waist with coins, then left the house. Pol pulled the door closed, taking a deep breath. The air smelled so different here, without the salty taste of the ocean. He had thought he would miss it, but he liked the woody scent even better. It felt solid and heavy, if a scent could convey such things.

The road below the house was busy. A carriage clattered past and the low din of voices reached his ears. As Pol was locking up, a flash of red caught his eye. He turned to see a woman dressed in a bright scarlet, tight dress entering the house next door.

"Good morning," he called cheerfully, adding a small wave for good measure.

He was thoroughly ignored as she went inside and slammed the door. Pol frowned. "So much for getting to know the neighbors."

Maybe the people on the other side would be friendlier.

Pol followed the road down the hill, not entirely certain where he was going, but determined to get there, anyway. He figured if he tracked the crowds, he would eventually end up in the merchant district. Their new house was in excellent condition, but Pol still needed a few things to turn it from a house to a home. And he really wanted to get started on the garden. The plants were calling to him.

Maybe if he made the place perfect, Nyx would spend more time there, with him.

Pol retraced his steps from the night before. The walkways grew busier the farther along he went, the houses once again growing steadily smaller until giving way to inns and taverns. He swiveled his head, trying to take in all the sights. Aleusia wasn't all that far from Parmouth, and yet, it was so *different*.

In a way, it was duller. The people here didn't appear to have the same love of rich and varied fabrics. Pol was beginning to feel conspicuous in his bright silk robes, out of place among all the brown, black and blue cottons and wools. The people of Aleusia seemed to have a liking for dark and heavy clothing, although that last part, at least, he understood. The wind held a sharp bite to it.

The hill leveled out. Pol looked back up the road and nearly groaned aloud. The grade was steeper than it had appeared from the top. He wasn't looking forward to going back up.

Someone rammed into him, and Pol decided it would be better to keep his gaze in front. It was a hazard he was well familiar with. Someone his size was easily overlooked, particularly if people were in a hurry.

Pol muttered apologies as he brushed past a large group. On the other side, he came to a swift stop, thoroughly impressed.

The road came to an end at a large square. A massive willow tree held court in the center, its branches spreading almost from one side to the other. Pol closed his eyes for a moment, absorbing the energy from the great tree. It whispered of age and power, of tears and laughter. Pol didn't realize he had moved until he felt the rough bark under his fingers.

He looked up into the sheltering branches, smiling to himself.

"Blessings, grandfather," he sent. The tree radiated surprise, then pleasure.

"Well met, child. Long has it been since one of your people have deigned to speak with me."

Pol didn't understand that at all. A tree this old, having spent so much time at the heart of a city, would be damn near human in intelligence and presence. It was only polite to acknowledge it.

He felt the soft hum of magic and the gentle brush of leaves.

"So far from home," the tree whispered. *"Be cautious, child of mine. Come speak with me soon."*

"I will," Pol promised, reluctantly taking his hand off the trunk. The tree's presence was like a warm, comforting hug, and he was loath to leave. But he had

a lot to do, and he wanted to be home when Nyx returned that evening, so he needed to continue on.

The large patch of grass surrounding the tree was scattered with temporary stalls and blankets, on which merchants had laid out their wares. The din of voices was stronger here, punctuated by the cries of the hawkers. Roads branched off several sides of the square, like spokes on a wheel, each one lined with shops, cafés and businesses. Pol picked a direction at random and began to explore. He passed a money-lender, a bookshop and a bakery emitting the most delicious scents, before coming to a shop that looked promising.

Pol spent the next few hours moving from store to store, collecting knick-knacks, pictures and throw pillows. He bought a basket, and quickly filled it, then a second. He finally broke down and paid a boy to run his purchases up to his home, keeping one basket behind as he continued to peruse the wares. The boy worked for one of the stores and, upon being given the address, looked at Pol strangely. It took a sharp command from his master to get the boy on his way.

Pol pushed the unusual behavior to the back of his mind and inspected the selection of fabrics laid out on the counter. He brushed his fingers along a lovely dark blue brocade. *This would make fantastic curtains for the front parlor.*

He began the involved process of bargaining for price, feeling that little thrill it always gave him. It was like a game, one he was very good at.

Pol obtained the price he wanted, grinning widely as the merchant wrapped his latest purchase.

"Thank you," he said, taking the package and adding it to his basket. "I don't suppose you know a good seamstress?"

The merchant, a portly man with a full beard, rubbed his chin. His blue eyes were startling in his dark face. "Lydia might do," he said, "but she's gone to see relatives. Won't be back till mid-week."

"That's all right. I'm not in a hurry."

The merchant wrote down the information to find Lydia, and that went in Pol's basket, too.

"What about an herb shop? Maybe one that carries plants? I have a garden that needs some work."

"Mackay's," the merchant said decisively. "Go back to the square and down Madderly Way, on the east end. It's the last shop before you reach the East District."

"I'm not certain..."

"New in town, then, aren't ye?" The merchant gave him a smile, which Pol returned. He'd asked his questions here, because this particular shop owner had seemed much friendlier than the majority. He, at least, didn't give Pol's bright outfit a derisive stare. "'Tis about four blocks total. The sign is painted red. Ye canna miss it. Mackay'll be able to help ye. And I'm not just biased 'cause he's me cousin."

Pol did miss it—he was on his third pass along the street and growing tired when he finally saw the sign, nearly hidden behind a gentleman's club. He took the small alley and found a doorway. There was no door, just a big piece of cloth covering the opening. Strange in Aleusia, but common in Parmouth. Pol pushed the fabric aside and entered.

The inside was so different from the outside that he had to stop and stare. It wasn't a store, but rather an open courtyard. Every inch was packed with greenery, pots of flowers providing a brilliant splash of color. A covered verandah ran along three sides, and more plants were crowded under the narrow shelter. The collection was incredible.

"I'm busy," someone shouted. Pol looked around, but didn't see anyone among the plants. "And I'll be busy tomorrow, too, so don't bother to come back."

Pol grinned. He recognized that voice. *Not Mackay, Mickey. Those accents will take some getting used to.*

"Mickey O'Rourke, is that you?" he yelled.

A bright red head popped up from behind a giant fern. "Pol? Good grief, boyo. What'cha doin' in Aleusia?"

"I live here now."

"Do ya, then?" Mickey stood, wiping dirt from his hands with a cloth. Considering the state of the cloth, Pol didn't think it did much good. "What prompted that, eh? Thought ye were happy with that bastard Jamal."

Pol shrugged, feeling his cheeks heat. "I found a mate, and he lives here, so I moved to be with him."

"Congratulations!" Mickey weaved his way through the disorganized mass of green to give Pol a quick hug. "Who'd ya mate?"

"His name is Nyx."

Mickey raised one bright eyebrow. "Nyx? Not Lord Nyx Contori, one o' the king's dragons?"

Pol nodded.

"Huh. How does that work? I've seen the dragons. They make three o' ye, little one."

Pol just laughed. "None of your business, you nosey old pervert."

"Old?" Mickey scoffed. "I'll have ye know I'm only two hundred and ten, thank ye very much. Old, indeed."

Mickey took Pol's arm and dragged him deeper into the artificial jungle. "I assume ye'll be wantin' to set up a new garden, then, aye? I'll want to see the space, o'course. Ye'll be wantin' plants to fit the space, mayhap a few from the coastal regions, lots o' color, if I remember correctly..."

Pol followed Mickey, letting the chatter wash over him. For the first time, he felt at home here in this strange city. He hadn't realized how much he'd needed to see a friendly—not to mention familiar— face.

"I always wondered where you went," Pol mused, fingering a lovely ficus. "You packed up and left so quickly."

"Ah, that."

If Pol wasn't mistaken, there was a tint of red on Mickey's broad cheeks. "Well, then, I had me a wee disagreement with the locals, ye ken? They didna like some o' my more...special wares."

"Were you selling hogsroot again, Mickey?" Pol asked with a laugh.

"Well, I'll not be saying I was, but then I'll not be sayin' I wasn't, if ye get my meaning."

"Ever the silver-tongue." Pol shook his head, delighted to know some things never changed. "Well, if you *do* happen to restock, I'm sure I know a person or two who would be interested."

Mickey would understand. Some towns were strange about the plant, Parmouth being one of them. Personally, Pol found a little hogsroot, dried and dropped into a tea, made a fantastic sleep aid. It wasn't the fault of the plant that some people were stupid, went overboard with their dosing, and never woke up.

That was the problem with people, Pol had long since decided. They didn't respect nature. They took it for granted, used it, and never acknowledged its importance. Pixies never had that issue. When you were so tightly tied to the earth, respect was inevitable.

"This willna do," Mickey suddenly declared, breaking Pol's reverie. "I'm going ta need to see the place. Shade an' sun an' all that good stuff. Lead the way, boyo."

"Now?" Pol didn't bother to hide his amusement.

"No time like the present."

"Won't your customers wonder where you went?"

"As if I care. If they get annoyed, they can find somewhere else ta shop. No skin off my nose. Ah, but we'll be wantin' this, fer sure."

Mickey picked up a plant bristling with purple flowers. The pot was large, the entire bundle towering over Mickey's head.

"Hyssop?" Pol swallowed a laugh. "I'm mated to a dragon. Summoning dragon energy isn't a problem."

"Never hurts ta have a little boost, now, does it?" Mickey gave a wink, then plunged into the greenery. Pol followed the bandy-legged figure, struggling to keep up and not get lost in the maze masquerading as a shop. It was a wonder that Mickey ever managed to stay in business, considering his laissez-faire attitude when it came to management. *Then again, he does always have the side business...*

Not that Pol would be talking about that one. Nope, not at all. He might not know Nyx as well as he would like, but Pol had the feeling the dragon was a little too straight-laced to be tolerant of some of Pol's more...liberal friends.

Mickey kept up a steady stream of chatter as they retraced their steps. The man kept trying to take the lead in their mini-procession, which didn't really work, considering Mickey had no idea where they were going. Pol eventually resorted to yelling directions.

"Left," he shouted. "No, the other left. Two paces, then… Mickey, look out for the lamppost!"

"I see it," came the cheerful reply. "No worries."

Pol shook his head and picked up his pace, nearly running to get around Mickey and the giant plant. He opened the gate along the side of the road and followed the path around his new home and into the backyard.

"Ah, this'll do nicely, won't it? But it certainly needs a Pixie's touch."

Mickey set down his pot, nodding in satisfaction, then began to pace the grounds, muttering incoherently to himself. Pol watched, a smile flirting on his lips. He stroked the leaves of his new plant as Mickey began making plans. One of the large, dark green leaves unfurled, meeting his touch. He let the leaf wrap around his fingers, listening to its song. He could feel the rest of the garden waking up, small tendrils of curiosity reaching toward him. The hum of life throbbed, growing louder. A burst of birdsong was followed by the low buzz of bees, and under all that was the soft sound of the plants themselves. Mickey stopped talking and tipped his head back, listening.

"Aye, that's the stuff," he whispered. "'Twill be good to have a Pixie in the city again."

"Wait, what?" Pol jerked, inadvertently pulling away from the plant's touch. "That can't be right. I can't be the only Pixie. It's the capital, for the gods' sake!"

The look Mickey sent him was one part uncertainty, two parts reluctance. "Well, as to that…"

"I *am* the only Pixie?" Pol found that hard to believe. And somewhat disturbing.

"Ye know Pixie's dinna like the city." Mickey seemed to be skirting the subject, and Pol narrowed his eyes at the man.

"Mickey," he said in warning.

"Ahh, boyo, do ye really want to know?"

"I think I had better."

Mickey sighed. Pol couldn't remember ever seeing a look quite like that on the typically exuberant man's face. Mickey sank down onto one of the plain stone benches and patted the spot beside him. Pol took the invitation and waited, albeit with impatience.

"Pixies often find the...shall we say climate of the city not to their liking."

"That isn't at all vague." Pol scowled at the reticent man. "Spit it out, will you?"

"The king isna overly fond of Pixies," Mickey admitted. "I'm thinkin' it has ta do with the whole mixin' powers thing, but there ya have it. He doesna run them out, oh, no. But they find life a tad easier out in the country, ye ken?"

"Great. Just great." Pol sighed. "And here I had to go getting involved with someone who interacts with the king on a daily basis."

"Yeah. I'm not thinkin' that was your best idea, Pol."

Pol stared at his feet. A small shoot was pushing up between two paving stones, reaching out for him. He sympathized with its struggle.

"I'm not sure it was, either."

But Pol was committed, and he wasn't certain that he could bring himself to give up Nyx, anyway. The dragon had managed to worm his way deep under Pol's skin, and Pol highly doubted he could be removed. Not without deep and abiding damage.

Mickey patted Pol's thigh sympathetically and went back to what they both knew best, plants. After a moment's hesitation, Pol joined him.

Whatever the problem, nature always helped.

Chapter Eight

Nyx stood on one side of the royal dais, still as a statue, and gazed impassively over the half-full room. Due to the size of the space, half-full was still far too many people for his peace of mind. Raven's, too, if the way the man prowled the perimeter was any indication.

Nyx cut a swift glance at the nearest window. He would swear that the sun hadn't moved in far too long. Then he grunted, crossed his arms over his chest, and returned to looking surly. He hated guard duty. Hated it.

Thank all the gods that Seamus only held open court two days a month. Any more than that and the dragons would likely revolt. Raven grew edgy and Kirit, in particular, got very growly. Of course, Kirit was always growly.

"Enjoying yourself?"

Nyx barely managed to keep from jerking. He turned a deceptively bland look on Raven, wondering absently if his earlier musings had conjured the man into being.

"What do you think?" he asked, instead of the curses that he wanted to let loose.

"I think... Hold that thought."

Raven strode off, his uncanny senses able to spot a trouble-maker before the person even knew they were a trouble-maker. His huge hand landed on someone's shoulder and he unceremoniously escorted the lanky man to the door.

Nyx wondered if he could make a run for it, but he had never abandoned his post before, and he wasn't going to start now, no matter how much he would like to.

Raven popped back into view. "Where were we?"

"I couldn't begin to guess," Nyx replied dryly.

"His Majesty needs to take a short break."

And there was another one who could appear out of thin air. Nyx, however, was immune to being startled by Desmond's unexpected arrivals.

"Lead the way," Nyx said. "Sorry, Raven. You'll have to lecture me later."

"Who said I was going to lecture?"

"Oh, please. You *always* lecture."

Not even Desmond could argue with that statement. Raven took his duty as leader of the Draak seriously. Too seriously, in Nyx's opinion, but the dragon was old. Ancient, even. Hell, word had it he was damn near as old as Seamus, and not many people could remember when Seamus had been born. Nyx figured the weight of all those years had long ago crushed all the humor out of Raven.

Of course, Seamus could still laugh, and he was older than dirt, so it was a rather shaky theory. Although of late their king had been damn near as humorless as Raven. Something was afoot, but as of yet, his High and Mighty Majesty and their Great

Leader had yet to enlighten their peons. Desmond likely knew, but Desmond knew *everything*. Cody had once said Desmond actually ruled and just let Seamus think he was king. Nyx thought Cody might be right.

Raven at his side, Nyx took a few steps along the large raised platform where Seamus was sitting, looking regal, cold and extremely Fae. He wore a stark white suit, in the style of Earth, the outfit making him look even more remote than usual. The white made a startling contrast to the deep red velvet of his fur-trimmed cloak.

Seamus always did have a flair for the dramatic.

The two dragons flanked the king as he stood. Seamus nodded his head in brief acknowledgment of the people still waiting to be heard. Then they took the short set of steps on the left side of the dais and went out of the door directly in front of them. Raven and Nyx hustled the king down the hallway and into a small, mostly empty room. The room contained only a sideboard, a long, low table and a matching pair of chaises.

Seamus dropped into one with a sigh, his heavy cloak billowing around him. The king of the Fae yanked the crown from his head and tossed it on the table with a loud clank. Nyx winced, hating to see such a pretty piece of sparkle handled with disregard. It was an impressive item, narrow bands of silver twining together to a point in the front, decorated at random intervals with jeweled flowers. Expensive, old, and Seamus always treated it like a gaudy trinket.

"I hate open sessions," the king complained, leaning back against the arm of the couch and tossing his feet up.

"Dignified and decorous as always," Desmond said, joining them and closing the door with a quick snick of the lock.

"Fuck dignity and decorum. They're worthless and irritating."

"You're in a mood," Raven commented, leaning against the wall and raising one dark eyebrow at Seamus.

"Sorry." The king rubbed at his forehead, and Nyx noted again how tired the Fae looked. "I haven't been sleeping well, and the ministers have begun pestering me again. On top of all that, tax season is coming up, and I have no less than eight nobles lobbying for changes."

"There is this wonderful new invention," Desmond replied, busying himself at the sideboard and miraculously returning with a cup of tea. The man was magic in his ability to produce tea from thin air. "It's called delegation."

He handed the cup and saucer to Seamus, who took it with a long-suffering expression. Desmond might have been magical in producing tea, but he was lousy in preparing it. The king took a careful sip, unable to hide his grimace at the taste. Desmond didn't seem to notice.

"I would happily delegate if I could find more than two trustworthy people in this entire damned castle," Seamus retorted. For reasons beyond Nyx, he continued to drink the tea, making faces the entire time.

"If you would let me—"

Nyx tuned out the familiar argument. He'd heard it, or a similar variation, at least once a week. The fact was, Seamus was a suspicious bastard, and Desmond was nearly as bad and never believed anyone could do their job without his input. Neither one of them understood 'delegation' and never would.

The sound of the king calling his name made Nyx startle, and he turned to look.

"You have been quiet of late," the king said. "Ever since you returned from Parmouth, as a matter of fact. Is there anything you wish to share with us?"

Damn, and so it starts. Nyx shook his head. "No, Majesty, just…preoccupied, I suppose."

"Oh? With what?"

"Nothing important," he hedged.

"Mmm." The way Seamus hummed conveyed his skepticism better than any words. "Perhaps a trip home is in order. I have been keeping you in your human form quite a bit these days."

Nyx knew that was a part of it and admitted it aloud. He and Kirit were both more dragon than human. He was used to spending weeks as a dragon, and not the other way around. Finding a mate had thrown his entire routine into a chaotic mess.

But he didn't want to leave his new mate alone for long, which kept him trapped in the city, leaving him with a seemingly unresolvable paradox.

You could always take Pol home with you, an annoying little voice prodded. And it was correct, but Pol was so…delicate. The caves were far from luxurious — it always astonished him that Cody, a human from *Earth*, for the gods' sake, had adjusted as well as he had. Nyx had this overwhelming desire to protect and coddle his little Pixie, and hauling him off to his stark abode… *No, it simply won't do.*

Kirit had always had a stronger taste for the finer things in life. His caves were well-appointed and comfortable. Nyx, on the other hand, was more apt to sleep on a rock outside, and had never put much effort into the little things, like decorations. Or a bed.

What could he say? His dragon was a tough bastard. He was the blocky powerhouse of their group, a far cry from Kirit's swiftness or Chaos' sleek grace.

"Then it is settled," the king announced, setting his cup aside with a clink and standing. "Once the session ends for today, I give you leave to go home for a few days. Chaos can stand guard during tomorrow's session."

The king snatched up his crown and plunked it on his head, looking far too smug for Nyx's liking. Then he swept his cloak into one hand and made his way regally from the room. Regally, and quickly, leaving Nyx scrambling to keep up with his monarch.

The man could be a complete bastard when he put his mind to it.

Nyx supposed he should be excited at the prospect of a few days freedom, but all he could do was fret over the logistics. Seamus would surely check, which meant going to the dragon caves several times...

I'll have to fly out, then back, then out again. Damn, but why have we been so resistant about a portal system? Seamus had offered several times to have a permanent portal opened between the palace and Benndragos. Clinging fiercely to their privacy, the dragons had always refused. After all, they could make the flight in a matter of hours. The isolation also made certain they weren't bothered unless absolutely necessary. But it definitely would have made Nyx's life easier right about now.

It wasn't only the comfort factor that had Nyx hesitating about taking Pol with him. If he did that, then he would have to explain to Cody. And, as much as he adored the dragon-mate, Cody was *not* the best at keeping a secret. He would tell Kirit, Kirit would tell Raven, Raven would tell Seamus…

No, he wasn't prepared yet to deal with that.

Nyx took up his position on the royal dais once more and resigned himself to a lot of traveling and very sore wings in the near future.

* * * *

Pol awoke to the feel of lips trailing down his spine. *When did I lose my clothes?*

Then those lips dipped down to brush against the curves of his arse, nibbling ever closer to his hole, and he forgot to wonder about his sudden state of nakedness.

"Oh," he moaned. "Nyx?"

"Who else?" The thought of another lover clearly had his dragon all growly.

Pol grinned into his pillow, then used it to muffle a shout as Nyx's tongue darted into a place that Pol had rarely even touched. "That's… Nyx, you shouldn't… Oh, Great Mapon."

Nyx licked again, his tongue hot and scratchy. Pol whimpered.

"Can I tell you a secret?" Nyx whispered the words against Pol's skin. "I like that sound."

"Not…not much of a s-secret," Pol replied, squirming as that tongue kept up its delicious torment. "Do that again, please."

Nyx obliged, tongue sliding along the crack between Pol's buttocks. The dragon nipped lightly at the small of Pol's back, and the sting sent the small bundle of nerves there into a frenzy. Pol wasn't sure if he wanted more or if it was too much.

"*Mellitus.*"

Pol loved hearing that, probably as much as Nyx liked him whimpering and squirming. It made him feel special, and like Nyx actually wanted him, specifically. Sometimes the mate bond could be a bitch. It left you floundering, wondering how much was magical and how much actual desire.

At the moment, with Nyx doing things to his body that he had only dreamt about, he felt very desired.

"I've missed you."

The confession took Pol by surprise. Reluctantly, he rolled over, but he felt the need to see Nyx's face.

"I've been right here," Pol said.

"But I have not."

Nyx looked...sad? His eyes were dark, and for the first time Pol noticed the shadows under his eyes.

"My poor dragon." Pol reached up and cupped Nyx's cheek in his hand. Nyx closed his eyes and nuzzled into the touch. "What can I do to help?"

Nyx pulled Pol's hand away, placing a kiss in the center of his palm. "You are already doing it. Let me love on you some more, yes?"

"If you insist," Pol said with an exaggerated sigh. "It will be a huge imposition, but I suppose I can let you ravish my body some more."

Nyx laughed and kissed Pol. "There's my Pixie," he said with delight.

"Absolutely. All yours."

"All mine." Nyx growled the words and nipped at Pol's pointed ears. "By the way, I like the hair." He buried his hands in the bright mass—which was probably hopelessly tangled at this point—and tugged gently.

"Oh." Pol had forgotten about that little detail. "Yeah, the hair. I was...bored."

"I am sorry, my mate. I promised to be home for the evening meal, didn't I?"

"It's fine," Pol hurried to reassure Nyx, who suddenly looked crestfallen, narrow lips turning down in the slightest pout. "You have duties. I understand, and I found plenty to occupy myself. Wait until you see the garden. It already looks so different."

"I look forward to it. Later."

Oh, that leer. Pol was already hard, but now it was becoming painful. He wasn't quite certain what to do about it, in all honesty.

"I need...something," he said, squirming some more.

"Hush, *mellitus*," Nyx murmured.

"I thought you liked —"

"Too much."

Nyx buried his nose in the space between Pol's neck and shoulder, sniffing intently. It was weird, but kind of sexy at the same time. Pol did some sniffing of his own, trying to see what Nyx found so fascinating. Nyx smelled like smoke, ash and apples. His scent reminded Pol of autumn, bringing to mind scenes of raging bonfires, crisp fall nights and harvest celebrations.

Where the heck did those images come from?

Then Nyx stopped nuzzling, started kissing, and all thoughts flew far, far away. Pol gasped and arched into the caresses, even as he felt a little lost. He thought he should be actively participating, not just lying still, and what was he supposed to do with his hands?

"Relax," Nyx urged. He buried his hands in Pol's hair again, massaging the sides of Pol's face with his long fingers. It was damn near as erotic as the kisses. "You're thinking too hard. You only need to feel."

"I don't know what I'm supposed to do," Pol admitted.

"I just told you. Feel." Nyx leaned in for another kiss, his lips hot and firm as they pressed against Pol's with sexy confidence. Nyx licked gently until he gained entrance, then began probing the depths of Pol's mouth. Slowly, Pol picked up the rhythm, tangling their tongues together. The advance and retreat had him humming in happiness. He let himself float on the sensations, his whole world narrowed on that one spot.

Then he realized he was rocking his lower body against Nyx's in a motion that mimicked the kiss, and that started to consume his attention. Pol would have felt embarrassed about such a blatant display of wantonness, but Nyx was doing the same thing.

"Taste good," Nyx muttered. "Can I...?"

Nyx trailed off, not finishing the sentence, but he didn't need to. The way he started tugging at Pol's clothing said it all. Pol had fallen asleep waiting for Nyx, so he was still fully dressed. Nyx had moved the robes aside to reach skin, but now he emerged and donned an expression of irritation.

"How do you...? Damn, this is a lot of fabric." Nyx eyed Pol's robes with disgruntlement, fingers fumbling for the ties that held the outfit together.

Pol laughed. "My big, bad warrior," he teased. "Defeated by clothing."

"It's ridiculous," Nyx said defensively. "You're wrapped up like a thrice-cursed Solstice present. From Chaos."

Pol didn't really know what that meant, but he let it slide. He shoved Nyx's hands aside and in less than twenty seconds was tossing the top layer of his robes aside.

"Wow. Magic." Nyx was clearly impressed. Pol laughed again.

"I've been undressing myself for years now, you know."

"Little imp."

Nyx dove for the first exposed patch of skin, pressing a swift string of kisses along Pol's collarbone. Pol kept wriggling, unlacing his tunic and working on the fastening to his trousers. The instant Nyx pulled back for breath, Pol yanked the tunic off over his head.

"Come on," he urged Nyx. "Your turn."

Nyx shoved his weight off Pol and stood, stripping his own tunic off in a casual motion. Pol sucked in a breath, impressed every time at the sight of his dragon's nude form. Nyx certainly had nothing to be ashamed of. Pol rose to his knees, still only half-naked, and scooted closer. He needed to touch.

He pressed his hands against Nyx, feeling the slight give of a chest that was more scales than skin. A deep, dark brownish-red, they seemed to ripple in the dim gaslight. Pol rubbed his thumbs against the darker skin around Nyx's nipples, giving the rigid nubs a quick flick. Nyx groaned. He licked his lips, and Pol couldn't help staring at the forked tongue. Nyx's eyes had shifted to reptilian, the pupils narrow slits, the color a deep, dark green—almost black.

It was the sexiest thing he had ever seen.

"You're so beautiful," Pol whispered.

Nyx shook his head in denial, but couldn't seem to find his words. Pol loved it, that he could have such a visceral effect on the dragon. Even though Nyx hadn't shed his pants yet, his erection was visible, straining against the confines of the cloth.

"I want to see." Pol moved his hands to the waistband of Nyx's soft leather pants, tugging urgently.

"Careful, little mate." Nyx pulled his hands aside, but Pol didn't protest, since he quickly undid the fastening and peeled the leather away. Pol opened his mouth, desperately sucking in air to his lungs, which didn't seem to be working correctly at the moment.

Nyx was a work of art. Large, strong, and oh-so-wonderfully strange. The pattern of scales continued down to his groin and littered the tops of his thighs. He didn't have a single bit of hair anywhere, not even around his straining cock. That part of him fascinated Pol. He reached out, touching the tip of one finger to the leaking head. Nyx closed his eyes and groaned at the featherlight touch.

"More," he ordered. "Touch me. Please."

Oooh, free reign to explore. Pol couldn't think of anything better.

He closed his fist around the shaft at least as much as he was able. He licked his lips, trying to imagine the fat cock spearing him, burying deep inside him.

He couldn't imagine taking that much hard, hot flesh into his body. But he wanted to experience it. *Oh, yes, I do, indeed.*

Pol dragged his hand slowly along the cock in his grip, afraid to squeeze. He didn't want to hurt Nyx.

"You won't," Nyx said.

Pol looked up, meeting the heat in those deep, dark eyes. Nyx smiled encouragingly, although it looked a little strained.

"Harder. Harder is better."

Pol took Nyx at his word and squeezed his fist tighter, loving the drag of skin on skin. He used his other hand to rub at the head, fascinated with the way the foreskin drew back. He had one, too, but it wasn't at all the same. Pol delved under the small flap of skin, touching the slit and coating his finger with pre-cum. He pulled his hand back and tasted. It was salty and a little bitter, but he liked it. A lot.

To the accompaniment of Nyx's groans, Pol leaned forward and used his tongue. His motions were tentative at first, but he quickly grew in confidence. It was easy to tell when he did something right—the volume of Nyx's cries increased and his breath sped up.

Meanwhile, he hadn't forgotten his other hand. He kept moving it, up and down, as he lapped at the throbbing head. He poked then, curious...went farther down until he could run his fingers along Nyx's balls. Thinking to what he liked, on the rare occasions he had pleasured himself, Pol began to roll the balls in their silky sac. Nyx started to pant, hips beginning a slow, shallow thrust.

"Please, *carissime?*"

"My pleasure," Pol whispered. Then, gathering his courage, he slid his mouth around Nyx's cock and sucked.

It was all Nyx could do to keep the roar in as Pol swallowed him. The blow job was inexpertly done, Pol hesitant and a bit clumsy, but it was, bar none, the best he had ever had. Nyx fisted his hands in the motley riot of Pol's bright orange hair and hung on, trying hard not to pull. It was a challenge. He wanted nothing more than to guide Pol as he bobbed, to thrust deep into the moist heat of Pol's mouth. But Pol was exploring with such eagerness, such enthusiasm.

"Oh." Nyx's mouth worked as he tried to come up with something, anything, to say. It seemed like he should talk, but his brain had shut down.

Pol pulled back with a soft pop. He looked up at Nyx, lips swollen and red, and Nyx lost the last tentative hold on his control.

This time, the roar emerged. He grabbed Pol around the waist and tossed him back on the bed. Pol laughed, the sound so joyous and carefree, and opened his arms in welcome.

It was an invitation Nyx gladly took, but even as he dropped down on top of Pol, he couldn't quite get rid of the caution. Pol was just so damn small, so delicate. His hand was quite literally half the size of Nyx's, his tiny feet barely reaching Nyx's calves as their bodies pressed together. It scared Nyx a little.

All right, it scared him a lot. If he hurt Pol, he wouldn't be able to live with himself.

"I won't break," Pol said, as if reading Nyx's thoughts. "Kiss me?"

"You never have to ask for a kiss." Nyx hardly recognized his own voice. It was a low growl, the tone sounding like he was trying to swallow a mouthful of gravel. The animalistic part of him was definitely coming to the fore.

He granted Pol's request, which wasn't much of a hardship. Pol's mouth on his aching shaft had been marvelous, but this, this right here, was quickly becoming his favorite thing in the world. The way their mouths fit together, the softness of Pol's tongue, the gentle way he returned Nyx's more aggressive movements. *Heaven*.

"What comes next?"

Nyx moaned. The thought that he would be the one to teach his little mate about sex was more arousing than the sex itself. He would be the first one — the only one — to touch that soft skin, to tangle his fingers in that wild hair, to kiss that sweet mouth.

"My mate," he whispered reverently. The impact of those special words hit him, as if for the first time. This was *his mate*. A person who matched him so perfectly. A person who would be by his side for the rest of eternity. The emotions nearly overwhelmed him.

"Hush." Pol was rubbing at his shoulders, crooning softly. "Are you okay?"

"My mate."

"You said that already."

"And I'll keep saying it." Nyx kissed Pol again, but the emotional moment was slipping away, lust overriding it. He had been able to shove aside the demands of his body temporarily, but his aching cock was trying to make itself known.

Then Pol pulled Nyx close and said those fateful words, "I love you."

Nyx completely lost the last threads of his precarious control. He growled, the sound feral, and struck. His aching fangs sunk deep into Pol's flesh. Pol shrieked, but Nyx couldn't stop. He hung on, still growling.

He was, at his core, an animal, and that part was overwhelming his more rational self.

Pol was still shrieking in Nyx's ear, but the sound was going from pain-tinged to pleasure-filled.

Damn it, we're not going to make it to full-on sex this time, either.

Nyx pulled his teeth free, tossed back his head, and roared loudly enough to rattle the pictures on the walls. Pol's own shout mingled, strangely musical.

"Yes, sing for me," Nyx urged. "Sing for me, *carissime*."

With another melodic cry, Pol came, the heat of his spunk spreading across Nyx's skin. The smell sent him over the edge and, with another growl, he added his own cum to the mix.

Nyx braced his weight on his hands, hovering over Pol, panting for breath.

Pol, the little imp, started to laugh.

"What's so funny?" Nyx asked.

"Us." Pol snaked his hands around Nyx's neck and pulled him into another melting kiss. "One of these days, we really need to do more than rub off on each other."

Nyx groaned, head dropped forward onto Pol's shoulder. And damn it, were his cheeks actually heating?

Shit, they are. I'm blushing.

Pol kept laughing. Nyx kept hiding. Pol tugged at Nyx's hair until he looked up.

"It was good," he assured Nyx. Nyx would have felt better if he wasn't grinning widely. "Sex with you is always good."

Nyx grunted and rolled over, sprawling out on the bed next to Pol. He glared at the ceiling. "That barely qualified as sex, damn it."

Pol patted him on the stomach. "Don't worry. You'll get it right next time." Another peal of giggles rang out and Nyx closed his eyes.

"Brat."

"Mmmm." Pol popped upright, kissed Nyx then climbed off the bed. "Come on. I want to show you the garden."

"Damn it, hasn't anyone told you men are supposed to sleep after sex?"

"That doesn't qualify as sex, remember?"

Nyx couldn't help it. A smile tugged at the corner of his mouth.

His shirt came flying at him, landing on his face, and the smile became full-blown.

"Get up, lazy bones."

"Oh, very well, if you insist," he said, the words muffled under the fabric.

Nyx grumbled, but he kept smiling, and he obeyed the orders of his pint-sized mate. He dressed, but only just, yanking on pants but leaving the rest behind. He followed his bubbly mate down the stairs and outside.

They emerged into paradise. Nyx froze, staring in awe.

"You did all this?" Damn, he was impressed. It had only been a day, for Goddess' sake. One day, to completely transform the space.

Only a Pixie. The garden was now brimming with life and color. Small benches hid in leafy nooks and the white rock paths were swept clean of debris. In the center of it all, Pol had replaced the fountain. Nyx couldn't even begin to guess where he'd procured such an impressive, artistic piece so quickly. A large, circular basin was surrounded by three mermaids. The carving was exquisite, the stone damn near alive. Water droplets, both real and carved, hung off the fan-shaped tails, and masses of stone hair seemed to move in the breeze.

It was impressive, and it made his heart sink into his gut. Nyx stared at the fountain and swallowed hard.

"Do you like it?" He looked over to see Pol intently studying his reaction. The Pixie was biting at one still-swollen lip, eyes wide and anxious.

Nyx pulled a smile from deep inside and held out his hand. Pol eagerly snuggled close. "It's wonderful," he said softly.

But he couldn't take his eyes off those damn mermaids.

Chapter Nine

One by one, the ministers took their leave. For several moments, the room was filled with the sound of rustling papers, the screech of chairs on the floor, and the low murmur of voices. Some paid their respects to Seamus as he remained seated at the head of the table and some simply glared, depending on how their personal projects had been received. Seamus ignored both reactions with an aplomb born of long practice.

In the corner, Raven stood, a silent shadow whose cold eyes examined each attendant with distrust. He took his role as primary bodyguard seriously, and was such a familiar sight that most of the time, no one even noticed his presence. People looked at him, but didn't see him, like a piece of furniture.

When the room finally emptied, Seamus sat back in his chair with a sigh. He needed the ministers, but that didn't have to mean he liked working with them. Pains in his arse, every single one.

"Ten to one the Minister of Science tries that experiment anyway," Desmond said from his own place seated at Seamus' right hand.

"Of course he will," Seamus said with a twist of his mouth that he knew barely qualified as a smile. "When has my denial ever stopped him?"

The Minister of Science was worse than the Minister of Magic when it came to experimentation. Or maybe his experimentation was more noticeable. After all, it had been centuries since Lyell had blown anything up, whereas Tostin had done so only last week.

"Speaking of, do the masons have that hole patched yet?"

"Nearly," Desmond replied, digging through the intimidating stack of parchment in front of him until he found the proper piece. "There was a delay in the shipment of Calcedon Marble that put them behind schedule. The overseer was most apologetic and promised to deduct some of the labor costs from the final bill."

"Generous of him," Seamus said dryly, "considering he's charging us the equivalent of a successful merchant's entire years' income for this one project."

"It's a large project."

"Raven, do stop lurking," Seamus suddenly said. "You know it makes me irritable."

"Sorry, Majesty." Raven didn't really sound sorry, but with him, Seamus never knew. Despite the fact that Raven had been with him longer than any of the other dragons, Seamus still found the man difficult to read.

"I have three more contracts that need to be covered today," Desmond continued, still in work mode. "And there's a letter from Liniard that needs to be addressed. Something to do with a tax dispute."

"Gods above, I hate tax season. Can't we dispense with it entirely?"

"Of course, but then you would have to find some other source of funds to use to patch the walls," Desmond replied.

"Never mind."

Seamus took the letter that Desmond handed him and scanned it absently. One year, he had tried to add up how much money it took to maintain his behemoth of a palace. He had quit the project when it began to depress him. He wasn't a miser, not even close, but the amount made him cringe. Whose idea had it been to build the entire damned thing out of marble, anyway?

Oh, yes, Father's – may the bastard rot in whatever hell he ended up in.

"Gods-Cursed Southerners," Seamus muttered as he finished the letter. "They're worse than the Northerners, I swear. At least those bastards are stubborn enough to handle their own problems."

"I'm not certain which is worse, myself," Desmond said. "Stubborn and independent to the point of troublesome, or needy and clingy enough to come to you with every small problem."

"I know which I prefer," Raven said, finally joining the conversation. "We haven't had a good skirmish in a long time."

"Blood-thirsty dragon," Desmond muttered.

Raven flashed a set of extremely sharp teeth in a mockery of a grin. Seamus resisted the urge to throw something at the pair of them.

"I suppose I had best return to my office," Seamus said with what he knew was obvious reluctance. "I'm sure my secretaries have at least three new emergencies awaiting my arrival."

"Most likely," Desmond agreed.

Seamus stood and took a few steps around the table.

"Majesty." Desmond stopped him and Seamus accepted the large stack of papers with a roll of his eyes.

"And you say you never give me anything."

"Oh!"

That tone...

Seamus came to a stop in front of the door. He resisted the urge to curse and stamp his feet like a child. He *hated* that tone. It never presaged anything good.

"What now, Desmond?"

"There are rumors, Majesty. Of a Pixie."

"There are always rumors, and I'm sure more than a few are about a Pixie. What makes this one so special?"

"He's a half-breed, Sire. And living in the city."

Seamus let out a violent string of curses. He dropped his forehead against the wall and cursed a few more times for good measure.

"I'll see if I can ferret him out," Raven said, tone grim. "Do you know where he is, and why he came to the capital? The Pixies, particularly the ones of mixed blood, usually avoid us like the plague."

Seamus preferred it that way, and it was something he had...encouraged, over the years. He wasn't certain if Raven was aware of that fact or not but, knowing the dragon, he was.

"Word is he's set up in a house on Lethia Lane, and he came here with a lover."

"On Lethia Lane, what else would it be?" The road was also known as Mistress Row. It had long been the favored area for nobles to stash their paramours.

"If you have to run him out, do so carefully," Seamus added. "The last thing I want is a lord or lady at my door, angry that I've deprived them of their newest toy."

"As you command, Majesty," Raven said with a bow.

"Dragons," Seamus said, but he did it with a smile. He stepped to one side to let Raven pass.

The smile quickly faded when he heard Raven bellowing for one of his men.

"Gods take the man," Seamus complained. "I don't need anyone dogging my steps every minute of the day. I'm perfectly safe within these walls."

Not to mention that he wasn't exactly without defenses of his own.

"I don't know why you persist in whining about it," Desmond retorted. "If he hasn't changed his mind in close to two thousand years, I doubt he ever will."

"Maybe I just like to complain."

"As you say, Your Majesty."

"You can be replaced, you know."

Desmond only smiled. The man's position was hardly in any danger. Seamus would never admit it aloud, but he wouldn't be able to run the damn country without Desmond, and his damned steward knew it.

"I need a vacation," Seamus said, finally going into the hall and beginning the winding trek to his office. A serious-faced soldier fell into step behind him. Seamus, with the practice of a long-standing habit, ignored the soldier's presence.

"Kings don't take vacations," Desmond said, following behind the soldier.

"They should."

"I'll make a note of it."

"You do that," Seamus said and picked up his pace.

"Stewards, on the other hand, take them all the time," Desmond yelled after him.

"Don't you dare," Seamus shouted back, ignoring the glares his undignified behavior earned. *Stuffy old farts.*

Desmond moved quickly, nearly jogging—while somehow still managing to look dignified—until he was walking shoulder-to-shoulder with Seamus again. "In all seriousness, Majesty, if you need a break..."

Seamus sighed and shook his head. "I am fine, old friend. Merely too many duties and not enough hours in a day."

"And difficult subjects?"

"That goes without saying."

"Indeed."

They reached the wing of the palace Seamus called home. He pushed open the first door on the right, entering the antechamber of his suite of offices—because he was king, damn it, and one office couldn't contain the sheer amount of paperwork the job entailed.

From their desks flanking the entrance, two of Seamus' private secretaries looked up. He had a veritable army of them, or so it seemed some days.

"Good afternoon, Majesty," they chorused in unison.

Seamus scowled. It was extremely annoying. It was his own fault for hiring twins. "Good afternoon," he said politely with a quick nod of his head. "Please file these," he added, handing half of his stack of paper to the twin on the right. Matthias? Malcolm? He never could tell them apart.

"Lord Gerard would like a meeting at your earliest convenience," the other twin said. "And I have some forms that—"

"Need my signature, yes." Some days, Seamus thought all he did was sign his damned name. And it was a long name.

He wondered what the reaction would be if one day he just started using 'Bob' on everything. It was short, simple, and honestly, who really looked at the things, anyway? Most of it was filed away in the archives, an absolutely terrifying warren of rooms that had swallowed more than one apprentice over the centuries.

"Desmond, would you—?" Seamus stopped and turned when the door swung open, nearly hitting him. "Yes?"

A wide-eyed soldier stood there, boots muddy. He held out a piece of paper with trembling hands. "General Mtalna asked me to deliver this, Your Majesty."

Seamus took it and dismissed the poor man with a quick jerk of his head. The soldiers never liked coming to the palace, and liked being in his presence even less.

"Desmond." Seamus walked through the antechamber and into his outer office, unfolding the missive as he went. "One quiet day," he said. "Is that too much to ask?"

"Yes."

Seamus scowled, not sure if he was aiming the expression at Desmond or at the General's note. "We need to get Marius back here," he said. "He's been spending too much time on the frontier. This thing is an incoherent mess. And why the hell should I care about a bunch of elders?"

"Majesty?"

Seamus tossed the paper onto his already cluttered desk and sighed. "There is, apparently, a small group of Pixie elders heading our way, if I'm reading the letter right."

"Pixies?" Desmond raised his brows. "That seems an...odd coincidence, considering our earlier discussion."

"I don't believe in coincidence," Seamus said grimly.

"I will recall General Mtalna," Desmond said. "Perhaps it would be best to keep him close at the moment."

Seamus nodded, barely noticing when Desmond slipped from the room. He rubbed at his jaw, feeling the slight scrape of stubble, and realized he had forgotten to shave that morning. Not that it mattered much—with his silver hair and Fae characteristics, facial hair wasn't much of a problem. Or any body hair, for that matter. It always irked him, especially when confronted by Marius' nice, fluffy beard and burly, hair-covered chest.

Just the thought had Seamus sighing happily. Yes, recalling the General was definitely a good idea. Not only could he use the support, but he definitely needed a little stress relief.

"Malcolm," Seamus called. One of the twins appeared in the doorway almost immediately. Seamus assumed it was the called-for Malcolm, but damned if he knew for sure.

"Yes, Your Majesty?"

"Have someone track down Chaos, would you?"

The secretary nodded and vanished.

Seamus had been putting The Renewal off out of respect for Kirit's new mating, but he simply couldn't continue to delay. The time wasn't ideal, but then again, it never was. He knew Kirit didn't believe it, but Seamus hated The Renewal almost as much as the dragons did. Having his entire personal guard go into seclusion at one time...no, he didn't like it any more than they did.

Still, it could no longer be avoided. No matter how much all the participants would like to.

* * * *

Pol sat up in bed, heart pounding. He rubbed at his temples and took deep breaths.

Damn, that was some dream.

He climbed out of bed, moving carefully so he didn't wake Nyx. He rather hated to leave the warm cocoon of the covers. There was a slight chill in the night air, and Pol would have loved to cuddle.

He was thirsty, though, and if he didn't go take a piss, there would be dire consequences.

Pol pulled on his robe. He tied it around the middle, casting a fond look at the bed. Nyx gave a loud snort and rolled over, but didn't wake. Pol stifled a small laugh—all he could see was the dragon's messy hair poking up out of the covers.

Pol made it out of the room without further disturbing Nyx. He took care of the most pressing needs then headed downstairs, still rubbing at his forehead. His head was throbbing and, while his heart-rate had calmed some, it was still rapid.

Why am I so edgy? It was just a dream.

A nasty nightmare, but still...

Pol paused while filling the pitcher of water. He closed his eyes, still able to see the scene that had awoken him. He had been standing at the center of Aleusia while chaos reigned around him. The night sky had been lit a bright blood red as the city burned. The phrase *"Niunoxtos crouo-samali"* had echoed in his head, though he had no idea what it meant, or even what language it was. And at the heart of all the chaos, Pol could see the willow, its massive branches turning black, the feathery leaves crumpling.

The willow.

Water overflowed the pitcher and spilt over his hand. Pol cursed and shut off the faucet, shaking water from the sleeve of his robe.

Unfortunately, now that the thought had occurred to him, Pol couldn't dislodge it. The faint buzzing in his ears was trying to render itself into words. Pol had learnt the hard way not to ignore it when something was trying to poke into his head. If they wanted his attention badly enough to test his shields, they wanted it badly enough to eventually punch through them. Pol would be the first to admit he wasn't completely in control when it came to some of his abilities. His shields weren't that strong to begin with.

Pol chewed on his lip, casting a glance in the direction of the stairs—not that he could see them from the kitchen. It was a reflexive move as he contemplated doing something he knew would make Nyx extremely unhappy.

In the end, the pounding in his head made the decision for him. Pol snuck back into the bedroom and grabbed the first articles of clothing he found, carrying them to the guest room across the hall. He yanked on the loose-fitting pants, then pulled on the tunic, only then discovering it was one of Nyx's. The folds of fabric fell down past his knees, and the shoulders kept slipping.

Hell, I'll be half naked before I make it down the street.

Pol didn't want to risk going back, so he improvised. He pulled the tie off his robe and wrapped it around his waist, using it to hold the shirt in place. It still threatened to fall off his shoulders, but the makeshift belt helped counteract the force of gravity, at least enough to keep him decent. He found a cloak in the front closet that didn't look like it would drown him and pulled it on. A pair of boots completed his oh-so-fashionable ensemble.

After that, it was a simple enough matter to slip from the house. Pol pulled the front door closed carefully, casting a glance along the street in both directions. As he expected, there was no sign of life this late — or rather, this early, since he could just see the first pinking of dawn in the sky.

He pulled the hood of the cloak over his head and hurried down the street. The footing was treacherous. It had rained during the night, leaving the already hard to see, uneven paving stones slick. He caught his toes once or twice as he wound his way farther into the city.

The tug was irresistible now. Pol moved faster, until he was jogging along, breath coming in short pants. He stopped just before the square to catch his breath.

Then he looked up and had to catch his breath for an entirely different reason.

It was glowing. In the dim pre-dawn light, the ancient willow was actually *glowing*.

Pol approached with extreme caution, because... *Well, glowing tree.* It was not natural.

As Pol crossed the grassy space, a guardsman passed him by. A shiver rippled along Pol's skin, because not only did the guard not seem to notice the glowing tree, he didn't seem to notice Pol, either.

A discreet pinch made Pol arrive at the unwelcome conclusion that no, he wasn't still dreaming. The grass was damp with dew, the moisture seeping through the thin soles of his shoes. His steps slowed as he neared the tree, every instinct he possessed telling him to stay away from the light.

The pressure in his head kept him moving forward. He could almost make out words now, the pattern that of a song or poem, maybe even a prayer. The cadence rose and fell in a gentle motion that he could practically see.

The leaves of the willow touched the grass in a pale cascade. The glow seemed to come at once from both within the thin stalks and from under the curving shelter they formed. Pol took a deep breath and brushed aside the curtain of white-blue, ducking a little to step into the canopy.

"*Finally.*" The whisper entered his head with the force of a shout. Pol winced and barely resisted the urge to clutch at his temples—he knew from experience that it wouldn't do any good.

"Is...is someone there?" he called softly. "I'm not... I mean...I received the call, but I'm not certain why..."

"*Only me,*" came the reply, softer this time. "*You know me, Pol de Maldra, Duke of Penoply.*"

"I gave up that title long ago," Pol protested.

"You can reject the title, but not its meaning." A tall, slim figure stepped out from behind the fat trunk of the tree.

Pol took an automatic step back, only stopping when he brushed against the willow's branches. "Who are you?"

"You know me," was that same damn enigmatic reply.

"No, I really don't," Pol replied, hearing the sarcasm that entered his voice even while he tried to stifle it. It probably wasn't a good idea to offend the mysterious person who could, apparently, make trees glow and speak into his head.

Then he squinted against the glare of magic, the light shifted, and he got a better look.

"Wait... Paul?"

The tree stopped glowing, the birds resumed their songs, and Pol cursed at his annoying-arse relative.

"Finally," Paul said.

"I ought to beat you with a stick," Pol declared. "What the hell is up with all the theatrics?"

Paul shrugged. "I needed to talk to you."

"What, you couldn't knock on the door like a regular person?"

"Where's the fun in that? Besides, I needed to get you away from that damned guardian dragon of yours."

"Nyx is my mate. Anything you have to say —"

"You really want me airing all our family secrets in front of him? Because I know you, Pol, and I truly doubt you've shared *everything* with your mate."

Paul said the word 'mate' with thick condescension. Pol wanted to hit his cousin, but that was hardly unusual. He and Paul had never gotten along very well, much to their parents' dismay. They'd had visions of a marriage alliance when the two were younger, despite the uncomfortably close family relations. They'd discarded the notion when Paul had set a pair of Pol's underwear on fire. While Pol was still in them.

Accidentally, of course, and he was ever so sorry.

Pol had gotten his revenge, though. That incident with the mud hole, the freakishly enormous pig, and the Baron's eldest daughter still had the power to amuse him.

"You're thinking about the pig again." Paul scowled, the expression sour and unattractive.

"Of course not. Although now that you mention it..."

"No. I did not come here to discuss that event, which you swore to never speak of again."

"Then why did you come?" Pol demanded, amusement fleeing. "Tell me and go away."

"I need you to come back home."

"I am home."

"Stop being so annoying!"

"According to you, I excel at it. I've been banished, remember? I believe the phrase 'on pain of death' was even bandied about."

"I can get the elders to change their minds."

That was something Paul had never understood — Pol didn't *want* them to change their minds. He was happy with his life — well, mostly. Sure, he and Nyx were having some rough spots, but what new mating didn't? Pol had no desire to leave his mate over it, though. And even before Nyx had arrived on the scene, Pol had had no desire to take up the role his father had left empty.

Pol wasn't cut out to be a duke. The thought of all that pressure made him shudder.

"It's your duty," Paul was insisting.

"No, my duty is to stay here and make my mate happy. You've delivered your message, you can go away now."

"Stop being such a brat!"

"First annoying, and now a brat. I feel so loved right now."

Paul growled in anger. After time with a dragon, it was on the pathetic side.

"You have to come home."

"You keep saying that. We could stand here all day, but it's not going to change my answer."

"The whole damn forest is coming apart!"

Now that caught Pol's attention. "What do you mean?"

Paul scowled some more. For the first time, Pol noticed the creases stress had formed on his face. His cousin looked weary, exhausted.

Afraid.

"What's happened?"

"Ewan—you remember him?—he took over as the Duke, but he's not being...accepted."

"I thought the elders—"

"Oh, the elders like him fine. But Faerie doesn't. We're having problems holding back Elithorn Forest. I'm surprised you haven't heard. A small squad of soldiers disappeared last week while taking Maddion Way between the village of Lian and the barracks of the Tenth Garrison. I don't think we're going to find them."

Pol wanted to curse. *What the hell, it's only Paul.* He let loose with a heavy string of profanity he'd picked up on the docks. Paul looked appropriately scandalized.

Elithorn Forest was home to a number of reclusive races—the Fayte, Pixies, Driads and Gnomes, to name just a few. They were all heavily magical, long-lived and well-settled. Over time, they had literally saturated the air with magic. The air, in turn, had saturated the plants. The nature in Faerie was already a touch more...alive than that of Earth. With the additional magic, the forest could almost be classified as a race of its own. It became wild and uncontrollable.

Seamus had stepped in when it began swallowing up entire towns. He was strong enough to beat it back, but it was a constant war, one he simply didn't have the time or energy to wage.

So, the title of Duke of Penoply was created and bestowed on the most powerful Pixie of the time. Seamus had done his special brand of wizardry and tied the title, the new Duke's life-force and some really strong magic into a nice neat bow. The Duke then had the power to keep the forest in check. The title — and that power — was passed down from father to son — and the occasional daughter — until it had been given to Pol's father.

Unfortunately for everyone, Pol's father had chosen to marry outside his race. The elders couldn't have the responsibility, not to mention the magic, passing out of Pixie hands. When Gerald de Maldra died, along with his foreign wife, they'd promptly banished Pol and handed the title, with all its attendant lands and wealth, over to a candidate of their choosing.

Elithorn apparently didn't agree with their choice.

"Just keep testing until you find someone the magic likes," Pol said. "I'm sure *someone* is acceptable."

Considering the expression on Paul's face, Pol didn't think he'd like what the other Pixie had to say.

"The elders did some research. When the magic was tied to the first Duke's life-force, it was also tied to his lineage. There can't be anyone else."

Nope, don't like it.

"Paul..."

"You have to come back! Even the elders are starting to admit it. If you'll agree to have a couple of bindings—"

"No." *Gods, no.* How could they even ask that of him?

"You can come home!"

"I already told you, I am home. Look, I understand it's a problem, I really do, but when you're dealing with magic, there's always another way. They're just going to have to do some work to find it." *And heaven forbid those lazy fossils exert themselves.*

"I thought better of you," Paul said, looking disgusted. "You're going to ignore your responsibility, your heritage, everything that your ancestors worked so hard to do?"

"They're your ancestors, too," Pol pointed out. "Why don't you do it and leave me out of it?"

"I'm not strong enough." It looked like it physically hurt Paul to admit that.

"According to who?" Pol asked. "You, the forest or the elders?"

Paul's silence was all the answer Pol needed.

"Interfering bastards." Really, the elders didn't know half as much as they thought they did. Just enough to screw things up.

"You're really going to walk away?" Paul sounded as if he couldn't comprehend doing so.

Pol didn't care. "Yep." Pol gave his cousin a mocking little bow. "Good luck. Have a nice life." *Just do it far, far away from me.*

He turned and brushed though the hanging boughs that had hidden them from view. He ignored Paul's attempts to stop him and began moving rapidly through the city. If he was lucky, he could make it home before Nyx woke up.

He should have known better. Pol's luck was never that good. Nyx nearly ran him over on the front steps. The dragon's face was set in hard lines, and he was missing a few vital items of clothing, like a shirt and shoes. But he probably hadn't noticed, because both his chest and arms seemed to have sprouted scales.

Pol didn't look too closely at his feet, thinking it was better not to know.

Nyx blinked at Pol for a moment after they collided, so focused that it took him time to recognize Pol.

There was a long pause, then Nyx bellowed, "Where have you been?"

Pol winced at the volume. "Hush," he said, grabbing Nyx's arm and turning him back in the direction of the house. "You'll wake the neighbors."

"Who gives a damn about the neighbors?" Nyx yelled.

Pol started shoving, trying to get Nyx into the house where the walls might help. Lights were already flickering on in windows all around them.

"Nyx, please."

Nyx grumbled, but allowed himself to be pushed back through the front door. Once they were safely in the hallway, though, he dug his feet in and glared some more.

Pol sighed. "I went for a walk." *Technically true.* "I thought I would be back before you woke up." *Also true.*

Nyx kept glaring. Pol always had been a lousy liar. All the recent practice hadn't made him any better. Nyx simply wasn't the most observant person in Faerie, which was the only reason Pol had gotten away with skirting the truth as often as he had.

"Nyx, it's late...or early, I suppose. I'm tired. Can we talk about this in the morning?"

More glaring, and Nyx looked like he had sprouted roots. He clearly had no intention of moving until he received an answer that satisfied him.

"I heard a call," Pol said. "I followed it. My cousin wanted to have a little chat, so we did then I came home."

"A call? Your cousin? I don't understand."

"It's a long story. He wanted something. I told him no. It's over. I'm home now. Can I please go back to bed?"

"Your cousin. At five in the morning. Outside. Why the hell didn't he ring the bell at a decent hour like a normal person?"

"Because my cousin isn't normal," Pol said. "Not even close."

Nyx sighed and, despite the sleep, suddenly looked exhausted again. Pol felt guilt stab at his gut.

"Please, mate, no wandering in the dark. It isn't safe."

Pol finally saw under the anger to the fear, and it made the guilt even worse. He stepped close and wrapped his arms around Nyx's hard middle. "I'm sorry," he whispered, pressing his forehead to Nyx's bare chest. "I just... He used nature to send out a call. It was in my head. I couldn't ignore it."

Nyx sighed but his arms came up to return the embrace. "Next time, wake me?"

"I promise."

That one wasn't a lie. Now that Pol could think clearly, he knew it had been monumentally stupid to go wandering around Aleusia in the middle of the night. This wasn't the tiny coastal town where he'd grown up, and where everyone knew who he was and wouldn't dare accost him. This was the capital, and any number of things could have happened. Pol wasn't helpless, but he was small. It was a limitation he had long since had to accept. He was always at a physical disadvantage, because *everyone* was bigger than him. Hell, even some kids outmatched him in height and size.

"I promise," he said again. "Now can we go back to bed?"

Nyx nodded, eyes closed already. "Sorry, mate," he said softly. "I shouldn't have yelled."

Pol gave him a little squeeze then stepped back. "I'm not so delicate I can't handle a little yelling," Pol replied with a teasing smile.

"Still shouldn't have done it," Nyx muttered. Pol wasn't entirely sure he was still awake. "Won't yell again."

Pol smiled to himself and started up the stairs, Nyx close behind him. Nyx would yell, but that was okay. He had heard great things about make-up sex. Too bad Nyx was clearly not up for it at the moment.

He got his dragon tucked back into bed, then just stood there for a moment, watching. Nyx had been asleep the instant his head hit the pillow.

Pol stripped down to his underwear and climbed into the bed next to his mate. It was already toasty warm under the covers, and he snuggled in, pressing close to Nyx's side.

He was tired, but he kept thinking about the conversation with Paul. It was, Pol knew, the first shot of the war. More would come, and they would keep pressuring him. It was another thing he and Nyx would have to talk about, and the time was fast approaching.

Pol propped his chin on Nyx's shoulder, thinking hard. Yes, it was time. He should have done it tonight, but...well, it was a conversation that Nyx should really be completely coherent for.

Tomorrow. Tomorrow, Pol would lay everything out for Nyx. *My parentage, my birthright, all of it. It's time for action, consequences be damned.*

He only wished he felt as brave as he sounded in his head.

Chapter Ten

"There you are."

Nyx froze, the pose screaming 'I'm guilty!' Guilty of what, Cody wasn't certain, but he was going to find out, even if he had to resort to cruel and unusual methods.

"Yes," Nyx said lamely. "Here I am."

The stand-off lasted for several tense minutes. Cody won.

"I need to go speak to Seamus. Again. He was... He has some papers...Maximus was talking about..."

"It helps to actually finish a sentence." *Yep, guilty.*

Cody skillfully and subtly herded Nyx into the nearest cavern, which happened to be the one where all the food was located. Cody couldn't bring himself to call it a kitchen — the walls were stone, after all, and there was nothing resembling a counter. Or a sink. Or a refrigerator. And the stove was a large fire pit.

Sometimes he really hated the lack of modern conveniences.

There were, however, several sturdy tables, and a large bowl containing some very delicious fresh fruit.

Nyx, with the obsession characteristic of all dragons, went right for it. Dragons were stress eaters.

"We haven't seen much of you lately," Cody probed with as much delicacy as he could.

Nyx shrugged, tossing a piece of fruit in the air and catching it.

Cody wasn't stupid. He knew a stalling tactic when he saw it. "Come on," he teased. "Spill."

Nyx looked at him with furrowed eyebrows, setting the melon down and focusing instead on the nearby pitcher of water. "Why would you want me to spill—"

"Never mind." *God save me from literal dragons.* "What have you been doing that's been keeping you so busy?"

Nyx eyed the piece of fruit. Cody snatched it away. Nyx shrugged again.

"Training. Seamus has sent me south a few times. Nothing special."

"Uh huh." And Cody was a pink-toed sloth. Nyx was a really horrible liar. He turned, looking for a place to set down the melon. The cooking area was tiny and space limited. Not surprising. Before Cody had come, the dragons hadn't done much cooking. They just went out and found a nearby flock of sheep. The thought always made Cody wrinkle his nose. *Wouldn't the wool get stuck in their teeth?*

"Hey, why don't you join—" Cody turned and realized he was speaking to empty air. "Damn it, Nyx." *When I get my hands on that idiot...*

A quick check turned up an empty hallway, and Nyx's rooms were equally deserted. The damned dragon had pulled another disappearing act.

"How am I supposed to interrogate him if he won't stand still?" Cody muttered to himself.

"Interrogate who?"

Cody shouted, hand reflexively going to the nearby stone wall to steady himself. "Fuck. Chaos. Where the hell did you come from?"

"The front door," Chaos said with a grin and a gesture.

Cody just rolled his eyes. That wasn't Chaos being literal. It was Chaos being a brat. "Nyx," he said. "I want to interrogate Nyx, but he keeps running away."

"Oooh, want me to pin him down for you?"

"If you can find him, I might take you up on that. Aren't you supposed to be at the palace?"

Chaos pursed his lips into a pout. "I was bored. It's no fun there without you around."

"Torment Raven. I thought that was your favorite pastime."

"Seamus has Raven in meetings all day lately. And Nyx is never around."

"Hah!" Cody exclaimed. "I'm right. I knew it. He's up to something."

"Wanna play spy?"

Cody should probably say no, but damn it, he was bored, too—and curious.

"Let me go check in with Kirit." The last time Cody had gone somewhere with Chaos and not told Kirit, the big guy had gotten all steamy. Literally. While dragon fire couldn't hurt Cody, that much heat was damn uncomfortable. He'd prefer to avoid it.

"You should probably tell him that Seamus would like you both to come back to the capital. He says Kirit has stalled long enough."

Cody groaned. And there it was, the real reason Chaos had shown up. He'd wondered how long it would take the man to get around to it. "It's about The Renewal, isn't it?"

Chaos shrugged, trying for nonchalant. He didn't fool Cody, though. Cody could see the hurt underneath the casual expression. "He doesn't tell me anything. You know that."

"I know. And I'll say it again—your king can be a real asshole."

Chaos didn't reply, not that Cody really expected him to.

"You might as well settle in," Cody advised. "If we're both leaving, Kirit will want to wait until morning. There's food in the kitchen if you're hungry."

"Food!"

Chaos was off with impressive speed. Cody shook his head. Dealing with Chaos was often like dealing with a hyperactive grade-schooler, but Chaos was infinitely more devious than any child Cody had ever met, with an evil streak that would do a comic book mastermind credit.

Cody ducked through the maze of rooms until he arrived at Kirit's inner sanctum. He blinked in the bright light, the sun glinting off gold nearly blinding. It took him a minute to focus enough to see the big, red-gold shape plopped in the middle of the room.

Kirit snorted, lifting his massive head to examine Cody with beady eyes. He shifted, sending cascades of gems and gold spilling across the floor.

"I still don't see how that can be comfortable," Cody commented, as he had many times before. But the thought of sleeping on gold and jewels...ouch. Hard and poky.

Kirit only grunted before laying his head back down.

"No you don't, big guy. Chaos is here, and you have to get up."

Kirit huffed, a small trail of smoke trickling from his nostrils.

"Don't give me that. Up. You've been basking damn near all day. Aren't you bored?"

The dragon rolled his head to one side, squinting at Cody balefully.

"Big baby." Cody went over and scratched the toothy muzzle. Kirit grumbled happily. Cody was careful to avoid the fangs. "Come on, up. Seamus wants us back in Aleusia."

Kirit growled, the sound low and irritated.

"I know. I don't want to go, either. But Seamus says, so move it, blubber butt."

Kirit roared.

"Tough. If you want to yell, you need the other form, and you know it."

A dragon's sigh was nearly enough to start a hurricane. Kirit heaved his big bulk up on four spindly legs. They really didn't look strong enough to support his massive frame, but they always did.

Kirit shook his head, dislodging a couple of items from his beloved hoard. Then the telltale tingle of magic brushed against Cody's skin. Instants later, he was looking at his Kirit. The big-muscular body begged to be touched.

Cody was never one for denying himself. He stepped closer and ran his hands along Kirit's massive biceps. Kirit smiled, the expression still toothy, and leaned down for a kiss. Cody lost himself in his big dragon immediately, like he always did. He went up on tiptoes, using his grip on Kirit's arms for balance, and opened his mouth.

A loud crash from the other room broke the spell and Cody pulled back with a curse. He had been looking forward to some hot and sweaty sex. After all, Kirit was already naked.

Unfortunately, they had a house guest who would *not* be ignored. And while Cody wouldn't care all that much if they had an audience, Kirit would go ballistic. Cody didn't want to explain to Seamus why one of his warriors was sporting bite marks and possibly missing limbs.

"I'm going to bite that idiot," Kirit grumbled.

Cody laughed. "Maybe later." He took another quick kiss. "We've been summoned."

Kirit sighed, but he looked more resigned than anything. They had both known this was coming.

Cody gave him a sympathetic pat. "I'm going to pack a few things. Why don't you go keep Chaos out of trouble?"

"Not even the entire Fae army could manage that."

Cody laughed again and smacked his dragon on the butt before heading for their bedchamber. "And put on some clothes!"

Kirit expressed his opinion of that suggestion with a low growl, but did as ordered.

Cody pulled out his bag then pursed his lips, trying to decide what to take. The Fae were also so snobby about clothing, but Cody wasn't putting on a pair of tights just to make the elitist bastards happy. He was firmly convinced that nothing could make them happy, so why bother? Besides, *tights*.

He did forgo the jeans, however, knowing that Kirit liked it when Cody at least attempted to fit in. And he had to admit, the soft, flowing trousers were pretty darn comfortable, even if he did feel like he was wearing pajamas.

A few tunics, some shoes that were more like slippers, and he snuck in his trainers for good measure. He tossed in the book he was reading then ducked into the treasure room to add a few of Kirit's favorite shinies to the mix. His dragon would pout if Cody didn't pack some, even though the dragon had another hoard in his rooms at the palace.

Cody went back to the main living quarters, then hollered in surprise when he smacked into someone.

"Damn it, Chaos," he grumbled.

"Need some help?"

"What did you do with Kirit?" Cody said, ignoring the offer.

"He got all growly and stomped out. I didn't spill the milk on him on purpose, ya know."

"Of course not. Here, take this." Cody shoved the bag at Chaos and went to dig up a few snacks for the trip. And some alcohol, because God knew, Kirit would insist on flying, and Cody had learnt that went a lot better with some whiskey in his system. What he really wanted was a tranquilizer, but they didn't make those in Faerie. Not any that he would risk using, anyway. Magic could have some nasty side effects.

"All set," Cody declared, brandishing the flask of whiskey in triumph. He stuffed it into the outer pocket of the bag Chaos still held.

It took him nearly five minutes to reach the entrance to the complex of caves the dragons' called home. He took his bag from Chaos again and left it propped against one of the massive pillars just inside the main archway.

"Now go make yourself scarce," he told Chaos, adding a little 'shooing' motion for good measure. "I have a dragon to cheer up."

"Have fun," Chaos said with a leer.

Cody just shook his head at the dragon's antics and went off to find his big, growly mate. He would spend the night consoling Kirit, and they could head for the palace in the morning.

With any luck, Kirit would wear him out enough that, with the addition of the whiskey, Cody would sleep through most of the flight.

* * * *

Nyx stared blankly ahead of him, not really seeing the wall in his way. He wasn't seeing much of anything, truth be told. His vision was fuzzy and his eyes didn't want to stay open. He desperately needed sleep. Pol's wanderings had disturbed his sleep last night. This morning, Nyx had attempted to retreat to the caves for a nap, but Cody had caught him. After making a narrow escape, there was no more time for sleeping, and it was back to the capital. He ached, his eyes were gritty, and nightfall was still hours away.

Raven's voice droned on in the background. Nyx propped his head on his fist and tried to focus.

"Nyx? Nyx!"

Nyx startled and blinked. It wasn't until he looked at Raven's stern features that he understood he'd dozed off.

"I apologize," he said stiffly. "I was —"

"Not here," Raven replied in a dry tone at odds with his expression. "Allow your mind to wander this afternoon, and you might find yourself with a few unexpected holes. Shall I tell the General that you will beat his soldiers into the dust some other day?"

"No, I am well. Simply tired."

"A tired soldier —"

"Is a distracted soldier, is a dead soldier. Yes, leader of mine." Nyx scowled. "I told you, I am perfectly well."

"Do I need to get Seamus?"

"Gods, no." Nyx waved his hand in a dismissive gesture. "Stop lecturing me, and I will be far more likely to stay awake."

"I wasn't lecturing," Raven said, offended. "I was instructing."

There was a difference? Nyx thought it was better if he didn't pose that particular question aloud.

Raven glared some more then picked up his 'instruction' right where he left off. Nyx let his gaze go unfocused again, but tried to stay awake this time.

Gods, but I'm exhausted.

He had never realized before how tiring it was, living a double life. *Or is it a triple life?* Damn, he needed a nap.

Nyx wanted to go home to the caves. He wanted his hoard and his rock. It was wide and flat, nice and secluded, perfect for sunning himself. Nyx could — and had — spent days comfortably ensconced.

He had spent far too much time in human form lately and his skin itched. Nyx wanted to go flying. He wanted...hell, he wanted his life back.

Normally, Nyx split his time between the palace and Benndragos, with more time spent at the latter than the former. But now, he had to add the little house in the capital to the mix. And Seamus clearly suspected something, because he had been pestering Nyx more than usual lately. And every few days Nyx had to fly back to the mountains and at least pretend to sleep there, or else Cody would become suspicious, and he'd rather try to fool Seamus. Cody was relentless.

"Nyx!"

All that back and forth, and the prevaricating, and Raven had increased the training schedule for new recruits, as he did every spring, and he hadn't been able to spend an entire night with his mate in the ages, and —

"Nyx!"

"What?" Nyx snapped.

Raven growled in return. "What the fuck crawled up your arse and died?"

Nyx took a minute to absorb the weird phrasing, but then he remembered that Raven had spent the time recently on Earth. He always came back with odd speech patterns — a mixture of old language and new slang.

Raven snarled and threw up his hands in a gesture more common to Chaos. "I give up. Go find Maximus. Maybe he can stab you with a knife a few hours early and put us all out of our misery."

"You're an arsehole. And I hate you," Nyx said evenly.

"I hate you too, *malum*."

Nyx stalked off while Raven laughed.

Maximus was in his usual place, standing on a box and yelling at a bunch of white-faced, bruised and battered youths. One of Seamus' generals, Maximus was in charge of the training yards. Waste of a good general, if you asked Nyx, but no one ever did. After all, it didn't take a lot of skill to force some basics onto the new recruits — just a really big stick. And a nice, strong bellow.

Maximus didn't have the stick, but he did have the bellow. Nyx could hear Maximus long before he saw him.

"You hit like my granny!" Maximus yelled at one poor scrawny boy. "No, scratch that. My granny hits harder! Take another run around the grounds, and don't come back until you've passed out at least once!"

The poor kid took off like a frightened rabbit. Nyx shook his head.

"You were obviously never told that saying about honey and vinegar."

"No, how does it go?"

"That you can… Oh, never mind, you wouldn't like it anyway."

Maximus grunted and glared. He was really good at both. "What are you doing here?"

"I thought I was supposed to be here. But if you don't want me…" Nyx made to retreat, but he wasn't fast enough.

"Hell, no, get your scaly butt back here. You can go show the Delta Squad that flipsy move of yours."

"What does that even mean?" Nyx wrinkled his brow in consternation.

"Pick up your feet!" Maximus shouted. "You're going to—hah!" He barked out a laugh when the target of his ire tripped over her own feet and went down in a heap, taking the three nearest bystanders with her.

"I feel sorry for them. I really do," Nyx said.

"Idiots, the lot of them. I swear to the gods, the candidates get dumber every year."

"Or maybe you get more impatient."

"Hah! Shows what you know. I've never been patient."

Sometimes, Nyx thought the only reason Maximus had advanced to the rank of general was because no one wanted him under their command. The officers kept promoting him just to get rid of him.

"What am I supposed to do again?" Nyx asked.

"Hold that thought." Maximus hopped off his makeshift dais and strode across the yard to lambaste someone physically as well as verbally.

Nyx thought about taking the opportunity to flee, but Maximus would likely just track him down. Or, worse, send the recruits to track him down. Poor bastards.

He gave the young man nearest him an encouraging smile. The kid was already big, and showed promise of wide shoulders and a beefy torso once he'd finally filled out. The kid made a strange squeak, turned an even stranger shade of green, and ran.

Maybe there is something to Maximus' 'idiot' theory.

"My Lord?"

Nyx turned with an inward curse. "Yes?"

The page gave him a sympathetic look and stretched out his hand, offering him a small envelope. Nyx returned the page's smile with a weary one of his own and took the letter. He ripped it open, scanning the contents.

I need you.

"Maximus, I have an emergency," he yelled across the din of the training yard. "We'll have to reschedule."

He left at a run, Maximus' curses trailing after him.

Chapter Eleven

The banging reverberated through the front hall, echoed along the walls, and thundered loudly all the way in the garden. Pol put down his book with an irritated sigh.

"It never fails," he grumbled. "Five pages to go and someone interrupts."

He carefully marked his place — he really wanted to know if Eliza managed to get herself out of the dungeon and married to Raul — and set it onto the bench. He stood, brushing out his robes. He checked his hair and made sure his ears were still hidden. Then Pol began the search for his shoes.

Meanwhile, the banging continued.

"Patience is a virtue," he muttered. "Now where the heck are my shoes?"

He finally found one embroidered slipper under a nearby bush, but the second one had vanished quite thoroughly. Pol gave up for the time being, setting aside the single shoe. His robes were long enough to hide his bare feet, and besides, it was his house. If he wanted to wander around without shoes, that was his prerogative.

The pounding grew ever louder as he made his way through the house. Pol was scowling by the time he reached the front door. He threw open the delicately carved wood and fixed a glare at the offending visitors.

A glare that promptly slid into dismay.

"Oh, by all the gods and little fishes," Pol spat. "What are you doing here?"

"It is a pleasure to see you, too, Your Grace," Elder Burkett said, giving a short bow. "May we enter?"

"If I say no, will you go away?"

The elder pursed his lips, looking frustrated and slightly scandalized, and Pol sighed. "I didn't think so."

He stepped back and opened the door wider, allowing his three unexpected and unwelcome guests to step inside. They examined the entryway while Pol examined them. Elder Burkett was the only one he knew, but the others were easy enough to read. Their reactions to the opulent hall told him far more than they likely realized.

The first one was similar to Elder Burkett, all duty and zero sense of humor. He reacted to the visible display of wealth with dismissive distaste. If asked, he likely would have called it gaudy and immodest.

The second one, Pol decided, was going to be even more of a problem. He had greed in his eyes and, while trying for outwardly impassive, envy on his face. This was a man who would sell Pol out in a heartbeat, if he thought it would advance his status.

"This way," Pol said, with great reluctance. He didn't want these men in his house. The sooner he listened to them and told them 'no', the sooner they would go away.

The parlor had yet to be redecorated, and Pol was thinking he might leave it alone. It was cold, forbidding and unwelcoming, perfect for making guests uncomfortable. He watched Elder Burkett settle onto a very rigid chair and hid a smirk. Pol hoped the loose spring poked the man in his bony backside.

"What do you want?" Pol asked bluntly the minute they were all seated, Burkett in his uncomfortable chair, the others on a hideous flowered settee.

"I see your manners have not improved in the slightest. Pity. Jamal was always so proper. I had hoped he might have imparted some of his mannerisms to you."

Oh, yes, let's all learn comportment from the owner of a whorehouse.

"My manners are perfect, thank you very much. I simply see no need to employ them with you."

Pol probably shouldn't take so much delight in the appalled look Burkett donned.

"This is a waste of time," the Burkett lookalike said, shifting his weight as if to stand. "He is obviously not going to cooperate."

"Give me a moment, Elder Lyonnes," Elder Burkett said, waving his hand at the other man. Lyonnes settled back with reluctance. "Young Pol might be abrasive, but he is a Pixie, and he will do his duty."

"I will?" Pol resisted the urge to squirm under the elder's steely gaze. Damn, it was like being a child all over again.

"I was told you spoke with Paul." At Pol's affirmative nod, the elder continued, "Then you understand our predicament. We are willing to reinstate you as the Duke of Penoply, with all attendant rights and privileges. The land will be returned to you, and you will be granted all access to the funds."

Pol ground his teeth. Burkett was very conveniently ignoring the fact that the elders had never had the right to withhold any of it in the first place. They were thieves, plain and simple. The de Maldra family had earned their wealth, and even if the elders could lay claim to the title, the rest of it was his.

"What's the catch?" Pol asked suspiciously.

"There is none," the elder admitted, although it looked like it physically hurt him to do so. "We are out of options and rapidly running out of time. The magic is not willing to accept a substitute."

"And when the king finds out about my heritage?" Pol said with disgust. "How long do you think your new duke will keep his title? Or his life?"

More stony-faced silence, and suddenly Pol understood.

He looked at them with cold fury. "I'll be damned if I'm going to lie down like a chicken in front of the ax. Did you think I was a complete idiot?"

This time, guilt replaced the masks.

"You did, didn't you? You thought I wouldn't understand what you're doing. You *want* the king to find out about my parents. In fact, I would imagine one of you will oh-so-innocently whisper the secret in his ear. The king will do your dirty work, and the magic will pick a new guardian. Well, you had best find a new plan, because I'm not going to cooperate."

"And how long will your cushy little position here last?" This time the third man spoke, and the amount of venom in his voice took Pol by surprise. "Your new patron will tire of you eventually, and then you'll be out on the streets again."

Pol started laughing and couldn't stop. Apparently, Paul wasn't that much of a snitch, after all. He had clearly left out a few pertinent facts.

"He's not my patron," Pol said with a wicked smirk. "He's my mate. I won't be going anywhere, and I certainly don't need your money, your lands, or your stupid title. So take your offer and get the hell out of my house."

Pol's bravado lasted long enough to see the elders on their way. Then he collapsed on the nearest soft surface and buried his head in his hands.

Goddess, what a mess. What the hell was he going to do? Because Pol knew, even as he'd rejected their offer, that he was in trouble. Big trouble. Massive, humongous, mountain-sized trouble. The offer had only been for appearance's sake, so they could claim the moral high road. It wouldn't shock Pol in the least if they went straight from here to the palace, telling tales to the king. Seamus wasn't exactly an even-tempered man, from what Pol had heard. And he wasn't going to be pleased to hear about Pol's existence, not one bit. Pol didn't think even being a dragon's mate was going to save him.

Pol shot to his feet and dug though the small credenza until he came up with a pencil and a scrap of paper. He scribbled a quick note and darted out of the front door. There were, as usual, a couple of urchins, dirty and of indeterminate age, hanging around on the street. He suspected that they carefully cultivated the image. A few coins, and one took off for the palace with Pol's note. Then Pol went back inside to chew on his fingernails and pace while he waited for a reply.

Nyx was going to be one very unhappy dragon.

Pol settled in to wait, but his book was forgotten and he couldn't seem to stop moving. His feet kept dragging him all over the house in frantic pacing, without any input from the rest of him.

"Stupid elders with their... How am I supposed to...? Damn it, what is Nyx going to say?"

"Say about what?"

Pol yelled. Without noticing, he had somehow ended up back in the garden, and now, Mickey was staring at him with wide, curious brown eyes.

"What are you doing here?" Pol frowned. *Was Mickey scheduled to visit, or...? Damn it, I'm all discombobulated.*

That was a good word, discombobulated. Long, flowy and accurate.

"I brought a present." Mickey held up a spiny plant by its thick stalk, bare roots still dripping dirt.

"I'm flattered," Pol said dryly. "It's lovely."

In truth, it was hideous, and more than a bit pathetic.

Mickey cast the plant a considering glance. "I know it doesn't look like much, but 'twill be a nice addition to the south corner."

"It had best not be illegal," Pol said. "Wait a minute, is that...?" He squinted. It was an immature plant, which had thrown him for a minute, but... "That's Valmaria."

"Perhaps." Mickey pursed his lips and considered the plant again.

Valmaria, commonly calmweed, while not *technically* illegal, certainly skirted the edges. Pol, at the moment, could care less.

"Hand it over," he demanded. He took the plant, wincing as one of the weird spines poked him in the hand. He fluffed the three pale leaves gently, then yanked one off.

"Hey, now, it's havin' a hard enough time as 'tis."

Pol ignored the protest and popped the leaf into his mouth. Valmaria was much more effective if you dried it and smoked it, but he was desperate. He chewed, the bitter taste making him wrinkle his nose. But the effect was nearly immediate, if muted. He felt some of the tension slip away, and his shoulders stopped trying to hide behind his ears.

"The south corner isn't good enough," Pol declared. "This beauty is getting a place of honor under the oak tree."

A loud bang reached his ears, and Nyx bellowed his name from inside the house.

"Better run along," Pol advised.

"I'm thinkin' yer right."

Another bellow sounded, and Mickey looked a little alarmed. Not that Pol could blame him. A panicked and protective dragon was best avoided.

Nyx came bursting into the garden with all the fury of an enraged beast. Pol stared, wide-eyed, having never seen anything quite like it. Nyx's dark green eyes were glowing, smoke swirling around him...and was he scaly?

Pol squinted. *Yep. Scales.* The skin on his arms was dark and armored, and so too were several patches on his face.

Damn. He probably should have been a little more specific in his message.

Pol hastily set his plant down and gestured quickly to Mickey. Mickey took the hint and made a hasty exit through the gate. Pol approached Nyx with the same wariness he would display around a wild animal. Nyx certainly looked the part. The low, steady growl didn't help matters.

"I'm fine, Nyx. I promise," Pol reassured. He took a few more steps, until he could put his hand on Nyx's arms. The scales were scratchy under his touch, and uncomfortably hot. "Easy," he said softly. "We're in the middle of the city, love. You need to calm down."

Nyx took a few deep breaths. More smoke filled the air.

"You needed me." Nyx's voice emerged in a nearly sub-vocal timber. Pol felt the words more than heard them.

"I did. And you're here now."

Nyx snarled. "Who do I eat?"

Pol choked back a laugh, thinking it might be inappropriate at the moment. "No eating anyone," he scolded lightly. "Although I reserve the right to change my mind."

The disappearance of certain Pixies would make Pol's life easier, but they would probably taste terrible—tough and stringy. The thought made Pol's laughter break loose, even as he knew he would never ask such a thing. He didn't want the elders dead, not really. He just wanted them to go far away and never come back.

And Pol was trying to delay the inevitable. "Come sit down," he said with a resigned sigh.

"Mate?" Nyx cocked his head, definitely looking more dragon than human at the moment.

"Sit," Pol ordered, pointing at the bench containing his plant. "And eat a leaf."

Nyx sat, giving him a puzzled look at the second part of the demand.

"Never mind," Pol said. He sat next to Nyx, close enough for their thighs to touch. Nyx was radiating heat like a bonfire. It was strangely comforting. "I had some visitors today."

Some of the smoke had dissipated, and the red tinge had left Nyx's eyes. Pol felt more confident now that what he said, Nyx would actually hear.

His belief was confirmed when Nyx reached over. Pol had been clenching and unclenching his fists in his lap. Nyx now pried his hands apart, taking the right one and lacing their fingers together.

"They made threats, didn't they?"

Pol gave Nyx a startled look. Nyx gazed back knowingly.

"How much do you know?"

"Nothing for certain. Merely suspicions. I know Seamus well, remember? And I am quite familiar with his stance on Pixies."

"About that." Pol sighed. "I'm kind of the reason he has that stance. Or rather, my abilities."

"I asked you a question some time ago, and you never answered. Will you answer it now?"

"Siren," he said softly. "My other half is Siren."

Nyx, to his shock, merely nodded. "I thought as much." He pulled Pol close, as if by holding on tightly enough, Nyx could protect him from all the dangers of the world.

Pixies were the one species encouraged to never interbreed with others. In most of the races of Faerie, when they intermarried, the offspring took after either one side or the other. Not so with Pixies. Instead, their magic stacked. They inherited the abilities of both parents, which gave them the potential for an incredible amount of power. The past was littered with horror stories of just such people.

"I don't have any desire for power," Pol declared firmly, not looking at Nyx. "And I have no intention of unbalancing the stupid continent."

"You could do that?"

"Probably." Pol sighed. "I sing, and the earth responds. I can't help it. But I don't really want to *do* anything with it. I don't want to cause trouble, and I don't even want to be a duke."

"Is that a possibility?" Nyx asked, arching one eyebrow.

Pol nodded. "My father was the Duke of Penoply. But the Pixie elders weren't any happier about my mother than the king would be. Jamal was a...friend of theirs. He took me in after their death, when I suddenly found myself orphaned, homeless and penniless."

And now Nyx was growling again. Pol patted the dragon's thigh.

"I don't care. I don't want to be a duke, remember? It's too much work. And politics. And talking to annoying people that I would rather just have you eat."

Now Nyx's growl sounded happy. It was slightly disturbing, if Pol thought about it too much. But Nyx was a dragon, and allowances had to be made.

"It's just...the elders came to see me today, and I didn't give them what they want, so they're most likely on their way to see Seamus right now, and..."

"Hush." The corners of Nyx's lips tilted up and he reached over to cup Pol's cheek in one of his large hands. "You're a dragon mate, remember? That affords certain privileges and protections. Seamus would have to think long and hard before doing anything irreversible."

"You're not really making me feel better."

"If it comes down to it, I'll take you back to my home in the mountains. Seamus would need his entire army to get to you there."

"Nyx—"

"I'll go speak with Raven. If we can get him on our side first, all will be well. Seamus actually listens to Raven. Or Desmond. Desmond would be good, too."

"Nyx—"

Nyx dropped a kiss on Pol's forehead and stood. "I'll return soon."

"Nyx—"

Too late. Nyx was gone as quickly as he had come. Pol didn't know whether to laugh or cry. "Goddess." He shook his head. Stubborn to a fault, dragons were. Yet, strangely enough, Pol did feel better.

He stroked a leaf of his new plant and smiled. "Well, little guy, I guess we'll let Nyx handle this for the moment. Hopefully, he can keep his scaly self out of trouble."

If not, Pol had a few tricks up his sleeve. He might not want the powers he had, but for Nyx, he would take on damn near anyone, including an arrogant king who needed a lesson on tolerance.

In the meantime, he had a plant to put into place, some pruning to do, a book to finish—and a shoe to find.

Chapter Twelve

"I'm not sure this is such a good idea."

Cody stopped fast and turned to look at Chaos in shock. "What?"

Chaos smiled wickedly. "I just thought it needed to be said. Now let's go before we get caught."

"Oh, good, I thought maybe you'd been spending too much time around Raven."

"Not even an eternity trapped in the same room would be enough to make me that dull."

"Thank God. One Raven in this place is enough."

"Two. There's Desmond."

"Don't remind me." Look up 'prissy' in the dictionary, and there would be a picture of Seamus' steward-slash-secretary-slash-God only knows what else.

Cody really was convinced that Desmond was the king, and he just let Seamus pretend.

"So where are we going?"

Chaos ducked around a corner and took a narrow path. It wound around the outskirts of the bailey, down the hill, and to a tiny door in the inner curtain wall. Cody thought it was kind of a security risk, but what did he know?

"I managed to track Nyx into town last night. I lost him a few blocks in, but only because that idiot guard waylaid me. I'm pretty certain he was heading for the residential district."

"You were playing detective and didn't invite me?"

"You were…occupied," Chaos said wryly.

"Oh." Cody smiled, remembering exactly what he had been doing. *Yeah. Occupied.*

The three of them had ended up heading back to the palace the night before instead of waiting for morning. Chaos had brought an amulet from Seamus, one that had let them open up a portal. One step through, and they'd been in the palace.

Cody needed a whole box of those things. He wasn't a fan of horses, and flying? That was on the very top of his list of most detested things to do.

Cody had thought Kirit would need to check in with the king, but Kirit had had other plans. He insisted they needed to rechristen their chambers. Cody hadn't put up much of an argument.

His smile was probably goofy, but even after over a year, Cody still couldn't get enough of his big dragon. And that big—

"You're thinking about sex again," Chaos whined. "You're always thinking about sex. It's not fair."

"You need to find a lover."

"I've tried. Everybody runs."

Cody laughed, then slapped his hands over his mouth and gave Chaos a sheepish look. They were supposed to be stealthy.

Chaos just grinned back. "The guards spotted us the minute we left the palace," he said. "They're just playing along."

So much for a security breach. Cody should have known better.

They left the palace walls behind and began the long slope down the small mountain to the city below. Cody was looking forward to this—he'd never gotten a chance to explore Aleusia. Kirit had always kept him too busy when they'd been at the palace, then they'd returned to the mountains.

Unfortunately, he didn't get much of a chance to explore now, either, as they started tracking Nyx. Or rather, Chaos started tracking. Cody felt kind of silly following after the guy. Chaos, on the other hand, appeared oblivious to the strange looks he received as he walked along, nose in the air, taking big, audible whiffs.

"You look ridiculous," Cody said.

"I know. Isn't it great?"

Cody should have known better. Chaos thrived on being strange.

"Huh," Chaos said between sniffs. "Wherever Nyx is going on a regular basis, he doesn't want anyone to know. He's going all round-about and sneaky."

"That's not like Nyx."

"Nope."

Nyx, like most dragons, tended to be direct and blunt. As Kirit always said, subtlety was for the Fae. Even Chaos, for all his devious ways, wasn't what anyone would call subtle. He liked to confound people, but subterfuge was not in his repertoire.

"Here." Chaos came to an abrupt halt. Cody, lost in his thoughts, trod on the other man's heels.

"Sorry," he said absently. "What on earth...?"

They had wound their way through a series of back alleys and side streets to a small row of townhouses a few blocks from the cities' edge. At the end of the row was a tall, narrow home, painted a dull gray with red stone accents. The house was built into the ground, with the first floor accessible from a set of stairs that went down.

This wasn't the high rent district. Even Cody could tell that much. The outsides of some of the homes leaned toward shabby and the gutters were clogged in places. The street was well-kept, but the residents had limitations.

"Interesting," Chaos said in a slow drawl.

"What?"

"This is the pleasure district. It's where all the wealthy stash their mistresses, paramours, and other various secrets."

"And Nyx is coming here often?"

"Yeah. Which makes no sense. He's not married, so no one would care if he took a lover. He doesn't need to stick them away out of sight."

"Then let's go see what has him hiding."

Cody should probably feel guilty about poking his nose in Nyx's business, but he didn't. If he'd learnt one thing over the last year, it was that the dragons often needed help. They were too…bestial. Normal human behavior sometimes escaped them. It was Cody's self-appointed duty to save them from themselves.

"So, frontal approach or sneaky?" Chaos asked. "I don't think Nyx is here right now. I can't feel him. We can either knock on the door or –?"

"Do you hear that?"

"Or we can do that," Chaos finished as Cody took off for the rear of the house.

There was a soft sound drifting through the air, hard to hear over the sounds of the city. The rumble of a passing wagon had mostly drowned it out, but Cody had been able to catch the tail end of what sounded like a lullaby. A lullaby sung in the most gorgeous tenor he had ever heard.

A gate at the side led into a lush, overgrown garden. Someone obviously spent a great deal of time here because, while the shrubbery was thick, it was also tended and kept somewhat under control. The paths were clear and the flowers blooming with vibrant health. Cody took a moment to admire—maybe they could hire this person to help the royal gardens. They desperately needed it. The foliage there always tried to eat Cody—literally in some cases. There was this one plant in the south end...

Cody rounded a massive rose bush and stopped fast. In the middle of the garden was a lovely fountain made of white stone. Three mermaids—no, Cody realized upon looking closer, mer*men*—held vases, water cascading down to pool around their curled tails. A shallow basin caught the water below. On the rim of the fountain sat a small man, nearly hidden within a swath of robes. Lavender with midnight-blue accents, the clothing made a fantastic foil for his wealth of bright hair. Cody had never seen anything like it before, the deep orange curls turning fiery in the sun.

Cody stepped on a twig and the small man yelped in surprise, turning quickly to see them. Cody got stuck on the mismatched eyes, one pale green and one pale blue.

"Hi." Cody waved like an idiot, hoping to keep the stranger from running. He looked poised for flight, all skittish and shy.

"Umm, hi."

Damn. *He* was the source of the song? Someone so tiny shouldn't have a voice like that.

"Hi," Chaos repeated, coming to stand behind Cody. Cody could hear him inhale deeply.

Then the normally easy-going dragon started growling.

"I'm going to kill him," Chaos declared.

* * * *

Nyx finally tracked Raven down in the small meeting room near Seamus' offices. It was a common enough meeting place, and he should have checked here earlier. It might have saved him the last hour and a half of wandering.

"Raven, may I speak with you?"

Raven was standing near the round table, gathering up a stack of papers. He looked up at Nyx's entrance. The older dragon didn't smile, but it was close.

"I wondered when you would finally come talk to me. Ready to unburden your secrets?"

"If I must."

"You'll feel better," Raven said with utter seriousness. "How may I help?"

"I've...I've..." He could do this. Just open the mouth and spit out the words. "I've met my mate."

Raven blinked, his few seconds of silence the only indication of his surprise. "Congratulations? Or are we not pleased about this occurrence?"

Oh, yes, definitely surprised, if Raven was pulling out the formal speech.

"I'm thrilled," Nyx assured Raven. "But there are some people who won't be quite as happy."

"Like?"

Nyx took a deep breath. The door banged open, and he sucked the air back in and choked. "Damn it, Kirit," he said when he could breathe again. "Knock next time."

Kirit cocked his head. "Why? The door wasn't locked."

"Perhaps we should take this conversation somewhere more private," Raven suggested.

"Oh, secrets." Kirit grinned, showing off his pointy teeth.

"Kirit," Raven said in warning.

"It's fine." Nyx waved one hand and considered his burly friend. Kirit was mated—he would likely side with Nyx on this issue.

"Nyx has found his mate," Raven said.

"Oh!"

Nyx found himself clasped in a tight embrace, one just shy of a wrestling chokehold. He made a weird gurgling noise as he tried to extricate himself.

"I think you're strangling him, Kirit," Raven said, amusement in his voice.

"Oh, sorry."

Kirit let go, and Nyx coughed some more. "Damn it, are you trying to kill me?"

"I'm just so happy for you," Kirit said with a huge smile.

"There are apparently some issues," Raven interjected. "Ones which I am still waiting to hear."

"Right. Issues. It seems that—" Nyx cut off the words when he heard shouting from the hall. Was that Desmond? Yelling? In panic?

Chaos stormed into the room, fury written in every line of his body. Before Nyx could blink, Chaos threw a wicked right hook. Nyx staggered back, touching his jaw.

"What the—?"

Before he could finish the question, Chaos hit him again. Shouts erupted, Raven and Kirit both lunging for their irate clutch-mate.

"You fucking bastard! *Ve'co! Cauaros ogros petrudecametos smertarvos!*" Chaos snarled. His eyes were glowing red, fangs prominently displayed. As Nyx watched, scales flickered across his cheeks.

Nyx gaped, trying to decipher Chaos' mangled Gaulish. *Giant cold...fourteen? What the hell?* He thought the last part was supposed to mean 'fat bull', but wouldn't swear to it. Chaos' syntax was atrocious, his accent even worse. Nyx was also at a loss to explain such uncharacteristic behavior. Chaos was, of the whole clutch, the dragon most closely tied to his human side. He rarely changed shape, and he *never* lost control of his human form.

"What the hell is wrong with you?" Raven bellowed. "Stand down, Chaos. Now!"

Chaos continued to struggle, intent on getting to Nyx and pounding on him some more. Nyx took a few wary steps backwards.

The door slammed open again and Cody entered. Nyx gave a sigh of relief. Cody had a calming effect on the dragons, and he could control Chaos in a way not even Raven could manage.

Cody moved in fast and landed a punch of his own, right on the same spot Chaos had already hit.

"What is wrong with everyone?" Nyx yelled, fingering his jaw and backing up some more. He had to stop when he hit the wall. "Why is everyone hitting me?"

"Because you're the biggest fucking asshole I've ever met in my life," Cody yelled back. "And I'm gonna knock some sense into you if I have to break every bone in your body to do it."

"Enough!" Raven's shout froze everyone in mid-motion. If Nyx hadn't been the focus of so much ire, he would have found the whole scene comical. As it was, he couldn't work his way past the utter confusion.

Then a small figure appeared in the door, and everything snapped into place.

"Damn it," he cursed under his breath.

"I'm sorry," Pol said, clearly frantic. "I tried to explain, but they were so angry. And they insisted I come, and—"

Nyx shook his head, cutting off the uncharacteristic flow of words. "It's not your fault, *mellitus*," he said, skirting around the others and going to Pol's side. He brushed a strand of hair from his little Pixie's face. "I should have known this would happen eventually."

"Would someone please care to explain what is going on here?" Raven sounded furious, and it made Nyx nervous. Emotion from the ancient dragon was never a good thing.

It was confession time—Nyx couldn't avoid it anymore. "May I present Pol de Maldra. My mate."

The room once again exploded into madness. Cody lunged for Nyx. Kirit hauled him back, the dragon mate spewing curses all the while, most of which Nyx had never heard before. Chaos opened his mouth, no doubt to add a few more imprecations of his own, muddled or otherwise, but Raven stepped forward before he could speak.

"I do not understand," Raven admitted. "A mate is a glorious thing, to be celebrated and shared. What made you believe you had to hide him from us?"

"It's not his fault," Pol said softly. "He was protecting me. I'm—"

"Hush," Nyx ordered.

Desmond slid into the room, breathing hard. "I have sent for the king," he declared.

Fabulous, just what Nyx needed to make this entire debacle complete. Pol's eyes went even wider and he began edging for the door.

"I'll just...you have things to work out, I'm not... I... Nyx? Help?"

Nyx put his hands on Pol's shoulders. "We are leaving. When everyone calms down, you may visit. Raven, if you would please accompany us, I will attempt to explain those issues I mentioned."

"No one is going anywhere," Cody said in a cold, hard voice. "Not until I get some explanations."

Squeezing his eyes closed, Nyx tried to rein in his own rising temper. "Cody, I consider you a very dear friend, but frankly, this is none of your business."

"I think it is. I know better than most how dragons can get when you latch onto an idea. And, like it or not, it's my job to remind you about being human. Pol is not some shiny bauble to be tucked away, and he for damn sure isn't something to hide. He's your mate, and that means he gets certain privileges, which you're denying him. He's not your fucking paramour!"

"Wait, what?" Nyx's eyes widened and he gaped. Then his mouth dipped into a frown. "What, precisely, are you accusing me of?"

"You're ashamed of him. Admit it!" Cody declared. "You hid him away like some dirty secret—"

"For his own protection—"

"—on Mistress Row!" Cody continued, talking right over Nyx's objections.

Nyx blinked some, anger slipping as confusion replaced it. He felt like he was missing a part of the conversation. A large part.

"We live on Lethia Lane," he said.

"Yeah, I know."

Chaos poked Nyx in the shoulder, waiting until Nyx turned to speak. "Locals call Lethia Lane Mistress Row, 'cause it's where the nobles tend to stash their bits-of-fluff."

"What does that—?"

"Their lovers!" Cody yelled.

Nyx was growing very tired of being yelled at.

"It's where they stick the mistresses and paramours. Ya know? The ones they use to cheat on with their spouses. The ones they *pay for sex*."

That last comment made Nyx growly. Very. "Are you calling Pol a whore?" He did some yelling of his own, taking a threatening step toward Cody, which made *Kirit* growly.

"This is getting out of hand," Raven said, shoving his way between the two verbal combatants. "Both of you, calm down."

Meanwhile, Pol had retreated to the corner, head swiveling back and forth as he followed the argument. Nyx wanted nothing more than to go over and cuddle the man close. Better yet, grab him and flee. Surely there was somewhere on this blasted continent where Seamus wouldn't find them.

"I think what we have here," Desmond said calmly, "is a failure to communicate."

"No kidding," Chaos muttered. "Take a deep breath," he advised Cody.

The irony was not lost on Nyx, Chaos being the voice of reason. That hadn't happened in...well, a couple hundred years, most likely.

"Talk to scaly-butt over there," Cody said.

"Why are you so angry?" Nyx asked, wrinkling his brow in confusion. He could overlook the earlier implication—this was Cody, after all. Nyx knew he didn't mean anything insulting by it, but dragons took offense easily when it came to a mate.

"Because he's your mate, and you should be treating him a lot better."

"I still don't understand what our address has to do with anything. It's a cute house, with a nice garden, and the owner left all his furniture behind, which means I didn't have to go shopping. Besides, Pol likes it."

"You don't—" Cody stopped talking and just stared, mouth open. Then he groaned. "I should have known. Damn dragons."

"Like I said." Desmond was most definitely smirking. "A failure to communicate."

Nyx saw Pol move out of the corner of his eye. When the small, soft hand slid into his own, he could actually feel the tension draining away. His shoulders dropped and he sighed.

"It's okay." Pol tugged until he could whisper the words to Nyx, "I don't understand, either."

"I thought... Look, Pol said you found him in a brothel on the coast." Cody was clearly trying to make a point, but damned if Nyx knew what it was.

"Yes," he said slowly.

"And then you bought a house for him that just happens to be on the same street where most of the nobility install their...let's call them lovers."

"Oh." Pol started to giggle. Nyx was still lost, conversationally speaking.

"Well, it was a logical conclusion!" Cody proclaimed.

"I'm still confused," Nyx said.

"I thought you thought that Pol was a prostitute," Cody said succinctly—or rather, not so succinctly.

"Of course he's not." Nyx would have glared, but he was still too confused to get truly angry. And really, hadn't Cody been one of *those*, once upon a time?

"Yes, I was."

Damn, Nyx had been musing aloud.

"You needn't sound so proud of that fact," Kirit said with a grumpy huff.

Cody rolled his eyes. "Back to the matter at hand. I *thought*," Cody said, dragging out the last word until it had about eight syllables, "that you were being a dragon."

"I am a dragon."

"Focus!"

Nyx thought he wasn't the one with a focus problem, but this time managed to hold his tongue, although he had to do it literally to keep the words from spilling out.

"It was, indeed, a logical conclusion," Desmond said with a nod. "You were ashamed of him, or rather, what he used to do, and attempted to avoid the issue entirely by tucking Pol away."

"That's ridiculous!" Nyx finally understood, and it was making him extremely growly.

Chaos started laughing. Cackling, actually, and Nyx really wanted to hit him. But that would mean letting go of his mate's hand, so he decided it wasn't worth it.

"It's not ridiculous." Cody frowned at Nyx.

Nyx frowned back. "Anyone with an ounce of sense knows it is," he declared. "My Pol is perfect, and innocent, and sweet, and..."

"We get it. He's the epitome of a mate," Cody interrupted.

Nyx nodded in satisfaction.

Unfortunately, just as he thought he'd gotten everything under control, Seamus entered the scene.

He took one look at Pol and his face went stony. Pol turned white, and Nyx's heart began a rapid thump he could feel in his throat.

"Raven," he said, warning in his voice. Raven, for his part, had one hand on his sword, but he seemed undecided on what to do with the weapon.

"Seamus, are you well?" Desmond asked, concerned.

"Everyone out." Seamus' quietly growled order silenced the competing cacophony of voices, but no one moved.

"I said, out."

Nyx grabbed his mate, more than happy to comply.

"Not you," Seamus said. "You two, stay right where you are."

"Seamus," Cody began, the only one apparently oblivious to the sudden rise in tension, "This is —"

"I know damn well who he is. Or rather, what."

"Yep, Nyx's mate."

Seamus eyes narrowed. Cody remained oblivious.

"Cute, isn't he?"

"Pixies typically are." Seamus didn't sound complimentary. "Go away now, Cody."

If Cody was ignorant of the rising danger, Kirit wasn't. He grabbed his mate and guided the protesting Cody from the room. Chaos hesitated, opening his mouth, then closing it before retreating, as well. Raven was the last to go, and only did so after Desmond whispered something into his ear.

Alone with the king, Nyx tugged Pol behind him. "Seamus, I can explain."

"No need. You find a potential mate, and in typical dragon fashion, didn't bother to resist the attraction, despite the fact that the potential in question was a

Pixie. And not a full-blooded Pixie. Oh, no, you had to go and choose a hybrid. A hybrid Pixie, Nyx!"

"He has a name," Nyx said harshly. "Use it."

"Do enlighten me."

Pol rested one hand at the small of Nyx's back and stepped forward. "Pol de Maldras, Your Majesty. And I want to assure you—"

"De Maldras?" Seamus let out a string of curses that Nyx had never heard before. Nyx winced. "Let me guess, my missing Duke of Penoply?"

"Not exactly missing," Pol said. "You see—"

Seamus interrupted Pol again, this time with a wave of his hand. "I've recently had a long chat with the Pixie elders. I suppose I should have taken them more seriously. They're just so damn sneaky."

"Elders usually are," Desmond said, stepping back into the room. "I've put them in the East Wing and ordered meals to be sent. I believe it best to try and keep the major parties of this little farce separated for now, don't you?"

"Far be it from me to argue with you," Seamus said sarcastically. He nodded to Desmond, who motioned to someone in the hallway. Nyx didn't think he imagined the extreme reluctance in Desmond's action.

Two guards entered, bristling with weapons and wearing full plate armor. Nyx swallowed a growl.

"I will meet with everyone tomorrow," Seamus said. "I would prefer to do a little investigating of my own before hearing all sides of the story concerning the duchy, the forest and the problems with the elders. In the meantime, I would request that you two remain in Nyx's quarters."

Seamus gave them one last glare, then left. Desmond looked at them with sympathy before following. The guards simply remained stony-faced, hands resting on the hilts of their swords.

"If you would, my lord," the one on the right said.

Nyx tightened his grip on Pol and stepped forward. "Sir."

The warning tone made him stop. Reluctantly, Nyx let go of his mate and raised his arms, allowing the second guard to divest him of his own weapons. When they went to search Pol, though, he couldn't stop the snarl.

"Easy," Pol said. He pulled a small dagger from his robes and handed it over. "That's all. I promise."

The guards exchanged glances, but evidently decided it was best not to provoke the already irritated dragon. They indicated that Nyx should precede them. Nyx grabbed his mate's hand and started down the hall, ignoring the stares and murmurs.

Pol gave their joined hands a little squeeze. When Nyx looked, he smiled.

"I can think of worse things than to be locked alone in a room with you," Pol teased.

Despite the gravity of the situation, Nyx's lips twitched in amusement. "I can too," he replied. "Shall I list them?"

"No need. Just promise me a kiss when we get there."

"Always, *carissime*. Always."

Chapter Thirteen

Something smacked Nyx on the nose. He grunted and rolled over, only to get smacked on the hip. He blinked blearily at the room. Dark shadows still clung to the corners, the barest hints of light streaming across the floor from the moons. The curtains covering the balcony entrance shifted in the gentle breeze, altering the streams of moonlight in random patterns. Nyx watched them for a moment, the sight strangely hypnotizing.

At his side, Pol shifted and sighed, arms flying again. Pol wasn't normally so restless in sleep. Nyx thought about trying to soothe him, but didn't want to risk waking him up. Nyx's poor mate needed his rest.

A shadow passed in front of the curtains, moving with purposeful intent. Nyx glared at it and rolled out of bed. The marble floor was cold under his feet as he walked across the room. A narrow opening led to the washroom, the small space only slightly warmer than the bedroom. Nyx lifted the ceramic flowered pitcher from its place on a stand and poured water into a shallow basin. He splashed the liquid on his face, then took a drink. He tried to ignore the soft sounds from outside, but wasn't successful. The brush of footsteps and the clank of metal would be inaudible to most, but to his heightened senses, they were as loud as a shout. Now that he had noticed them, he couldn't filter them out.

Nyx braced his arms on the table in front of him, staring blankly at the still surface of the water. When he closed his eyes, he could see the warm glow of lamplight and rich red bedding, his pixie sprawled in the nest made by the coverings.

He wanted to go home. Strange, how so much had changed, so quickly. He had spent centuries moving between the caves in the mountains and this very suite of rooms in the palace and yet, when he thought of home now, all he could see was the little house in town. Nyx wanted to wake Pol and take him back, to their cozy rooms and lush garden.

Too bad they were under arrest.

Oh, Seamus had been diplomatic about it, expressing concern over the Pixie elders' machinations, worrying about the unstable duchy. Nyx wasn't fooled. He had seen the distrust in the king's eyes. Seamus' face had been cold and hard, every line in his body screaming his royalty. The monarch was in control and would brook no threat to his reign. Not that Pol was a threat, but Seamus wasn't inclined to listen. Only time would prove the truth, time Nyx wasn't certain they had.

Another sound caught his attention, louder and more purposeful than those made by the guards stationed outside their rooms. Nyx stood, wishing in vain for his weapons, the ones that had been stripped from the rooms earlier that day. Still, he was a dragon.

Weapons made him happy, but they weren't truly necessary.

A few quick strides took him back through the bedroom. The sounds had come from the balcony, and Nyx pushed through the curtains with determination, claws extended and a growl rumbling in his throat.

"Peace, brother."

Nyx stopped mid-stride as Raven stepped from the shadows, but he didn't relax his stance, or retract his claws.

"What do you want?"

Raven sighed, the sound weary. He leaned back against the railing encircling the small balcony and studied Nyx with penetrating eyes, eyes that were darker than normal. Nyx knew that look and could feel it burrowing deep into his soul. His commander possessed a great deal of power, although he generally preferred not to exercise it. Circumstances didn't often call for it, not in their quiet world.

What Nyx didn't sense was a threat. He heaved a sigh of his own, sheathed his claws, and joined Raven at the railing.

"What news?" he asked quietly, not wanting to disturb Pol.

"I've been arguing with the stubborn idiot for hours, but he isn't budging." Raven rubbed at the back of his neck, an uncharacteristically telling motion.

"Is my mate in danger?"

Raven shook his head. "Not at the moment."

Nyx stared hard, trying to discern the truth. He trusted Raven, but the older dragon's first loyalty had always been to the king.

Raven looked hurt at the scrutiny, which was likely tinged with distrust. "I am loyal," he said around a growl, "but not blindly so. Anyone can see that Pol is passive, submissive, and not in the least bit ambitious. Seamus' paranoia is groundless, and if he would pull his head out of his arse, he would see it. He *will* move past this, just give him time."

"How much time?" Nyx demanded. "How long will we be locked up like traitors? I have served him for centuries, my commitment should not be questioned. I have accepted Pol as my mate. Seamus should trust me enough to know I would never do so if I weren't convinced of Pol's sincerity. His bloodline is hardly his fault."

"You know trust has always been an issue with Seamus. Too many betrayals at too young an age made him cynical, but he does have faith in his dragons. He *will* change his mind."

"And if he doesn't?" Nyx didn't even want to think it, let alone voice it, but the problem had to be addressed. "If he won't see reason?"

"He will." Raven's words were buried under a growl, the dragon impatient with Nyx's pushing. "You know Seamus."

"I do, but—"

"He's only concerned because he knows how obsessive we can become over mates. Once he understands that your insistence isn't due to a dragon's short-sighted possessiveness, he'll relent."

"So now I'm an idiot. Is that it?"

"Nyx."

It wasn't until he heard his name called that Nyx realized he was yelling. Pol stepped onto the balcony, and Nyx immediately felt guilty.

"I'm sorry, *mellitus*. I didn't mean to wake you."

"It's fine. I wasn't sleeping well, anyway."

And now he felt even guiltier.

"Oh, stop it," Pol scolded gently. "This was going to happen eventually, whether you mated me or not."

"Quite right," Raven said. "I am amazed, in fact, that Seamus was not made aware of your parentage earlier. He is typically far more in tune with his populace than that."

"He's been distracted of late."

"Mmmm. The ministers and nobility have been...pushing. But that is neither here nor there." Raven smiled at Pol, which took Nyx by surprise. Then again, if anyone could soften Raven's hard exterior, it would be Pol. "Worry not, little one. Simply enjoy your time alone with your mate. I fear it is something we dragons have little enough of. And with The Renewal approaching—"

"Damn it, Raven!"

"Oops."

Raven didn't look the least bit apologetic for spilling the news Nyx had been avoiding.

"What's The Renewal?" Pol moved closer to Nyx. Nyx draped his arm over his mate's shoulders, drawing a hum of happiness from Pol. It was astonishing how simply touching his mate was enough to calm the ragged edges of his temper.

Unfortunately, he still needed to answer Pol's question.

"The Renewal is a ritual performed every several hundred years. It involves the dragons going into seclusion."

"How long?"

"Two months."

Even as Nyx said it, Raven was shaking his head.

"That's not quite right. The last time, it took two months, but the length varies. The first Renewal took nearly six."

"Six?" Nyx's voice came out strangled as he stared in horror at Raven. "I've never heard... Six?"

He wanted to whimper. Away from his mate for six whole months?

"No one is saying it will take six months," Raven hastened to assure them. "I only wanted to point out that... Hell, I should probably just shut up now."

"Please do," Nyx said, glaring at his commander.

"If it takes that long, then there's little enough we can do about it," Pol said with his usual pragmatism. "No sense panicking over it. Come, mate. It's late. Or early, depending on your point of view, I suppose. Back to bed with you."

"I'm not tired," Nyx protested.

"I said back to bed, not back to sleep."

Nyx wasted no time in following his mate indoors, but paused again when Raven called his name.

"What's the other part?" he asked. "Pol, I mean."

Nyx shook his head. "No. You may trust Seamus, but at the moment, I'm not certain I do. He'll learn the truth eventually, but I would prefer it happen once some of the edges of his anger have softened. If he learnt now, I believe neither Pol nor I would live to see the morning."

"Siren, then."

"Goddess damn you, Raven," Nyx retorted, but without any heat. Raven smirked.

"As you say, Seamus will find out soon enough. But not from me. Go enjoy your mate."

Pol pulled the gauzy drapes closed behind Nyx, covering the room in a pale blue haze. It was bright out there, between the full moons and the periodic magic-fueled torch used to illuminate the grounds.

"I believe you said something about bed?"

177

Nyx whispered the words in Pol's ear, his breath warm on his Pol's skin. Pol suppressed a shiver—the good kind.

Pol dropped his head back, resting his weight on Nyx's chest. The dragon's size comforted him, made him feel surrounded and protected.

"Are you ashamed of me?"

Shit, he hadn't meant to say that. Pol bit his lip. He wanted to call the words back, but they were out, and truly, he couldn't regret it. He had been thinking about it ever since the day before, when Cody had brought up the issue. Before then, it had merely been a niggling uncertainty in the back of his head. Now, it was screaming at him, and he couldn't ignore it.

Nyx tugged Pol around, staring at him in the dim light. "What? No, I... Why would you ask such a thing?"

"I thought... It's not important." Pol tried to brush it aside, but Nyx persisted with typical dragon obstinacy.

"If it weren't important, you wouldn't have said it. Whatever would make you think I am ashamed of you?"

Pol looked away from Nyx's penetrating stare. "There's the whole brothel thing. And the Siren thing. It's—"

"Ridiculous." Nyx frowned. "Working in a brothel is nothing to be concerned about, particularly as you could have performed the same duties in damn near any inn or tavern in the country. As for the Siren, that is hardly your fault. Besides, if you weren't part Siren, you wouldn't be the Pol that I know and... Goddess take it. That I know and love."

"Love?"

The world froze. Pol couldn't take his eyes off Nyx. Nyx, for his part, looked grumpy and somewhat constipated. True, Pol had known that Nyx cared. He called him *carissime*, after all. Pol had noticed, when the endearments had switched from 'Honey' to 'Love'.

But to actually hear the words spoken out loud...

"Of course I do," Nyx said, although the words seemed to stick a little in his throat.

"You...you haven't claimed me," Pol said in a near whisper. "I mean, you've acknowledged me as your mate, but you haven't...finished it. The bite and the sex and the *ceremony* of it."

Of all the reactions Pol expected, the deep and sudden blush was the last one. Pol watched in amazement as the color started in Nyx's cheeks and spread until even the tips of his ears were tinted. Nyx looked down at his feet, reminding Pol of nothing so much as a shy little boy.

"Nyx?" A smile tugged at the corner of Pol's mouth. He stood on tiptoe and brushed strands of dark blond hair away from Nyx's darkening eyes. "Talk to me, please."

"It has nothing to do with you. I promise. I... Wait, are you taller?"

"And it only took you a solid week to notice," Pol said wryly. "Siren, remember? Shape-changer? I can't consciously control it, but subconsciously? Absolutely. I have no idea where the orange hair and the curls came from, but the extra inches of height? Oh, yes, that one is all your fault."

Pol smiled to show he wasn't annoyed. Actually, it was kind of nice. It wasn't a lot of height, but it made him feel less like a child when he stood next to his giant dragon mate.

"You're still tiny."

"I'll always be tiny. Oh, great Goddess, don't tell me that's what this is all about?"

"I don't want to hurt you," Nyx whispered.

Pol pushed on Nyx's chest, moving them backwards until Nyx's knees hit the bed. The dragon sat down heavily and Pol followed, perching himself on Nyx's lap. He dug his fingers into Nyx's hair, pulling until he could look into his mate's eyes.

"You would never hurt me. Never."

"Pol—"

"Nope. Not happening." Then he leaned forward and nuzzled against Nyx's ear. "Besides, who said you would be on top?"

Nyx's groan was immediate. "Don't... Would you really...? I want that. Please."

"Lie back, love."

Nyx obeyed with satisfying alacrity. He did want this. Pol hadn't dared to hope.

Before following, Pol stripped his clothes off, tossing them to one side. Nyx gave a strangled groan and reached to touch all the bared skin. Pol slapped his hands away.

"Patience," he said. Oh, yes, he was liking this control thing.

Nyx growled. He liked that too.

Pol tried for stern and dominant. He lasted through stripping Nyx of his clothes. Then he started giggling.

"I've had many reactions to my naked body," Nyx commented dryly. "But laughter is a new one."

"Sorry," Pol said around his laughter. "Sorry."

Nyx growled again, the sound light and happy. He grabbed Pol around the waist and swung him around, pinning him to the bed. He went right for the sensitive spots, digging his fingers in and tickling without mercy. Pol shrieked, laughing so hard he could barely breathe.

"Little brat." Nyx's smile was huge, his eyes bright with mirth. At least he stopped tickling.

"Your little brat." Pol was breathing heavily. He reached up and placed a kiss on the end of Nyx's pointed nose.

"You missed."

"Did I? I guess I'll have to try again." Pol hooked his arms around Nyx's neck and tugged. He loved the feeling of Nyx plastered on top of him, pressing close from…well, head to toe on Pol, anyway. For Nyx, it was more like knee to chest. And Nyx had to brace his weight, because if he slipped, Pol would end up very flat. It would possibly be fatal.

"I love your kisses," Nyx admitted.

"You can have as many as you want." Pol followed his words with actions. He loved it, too. The feel of Nyx's chapped lips, the brush of skin, the softness of his tongue and the sharp points of his fangs. Pol ran the end of his own tongue along one of those fangs, glorying in the shudder that ran through Nyx. He did it again, and again, until Nyx was moaning happily.

They broke the kiss long enough to divest Pol of his own clothing, and that was even better. Skin to skin, the burning heat and the almost harsh scrape of scales as Nyx's control slipped.

"Claim me?" Pol begged.

Nyx didn't answer, but his hum made pleasurable tingles pop up along Pol's skin. Nyx rolled them again, until Pol was once more on top.

"Don't want to squish the little pixie," he teased.

"Nope. That might put a damper on the evening's activities."

"Technically, it's morning."

"Semantics." Pol took another kiss. As much as he liked being under Nyx, he liked this more. He felt safe and supported, surrounded by his dragon's heat and power.

"Slick stuff," Nyx reminded him.

"Where did you put it?"

Nyx frowned, brow furrowing in sudden annoyance. "Damned if I know."

"Marvelous." Putting his palms flat on Nyx's chest, Pol levered himself up. "Nothing interrupts the moment more than having to hunt for the oil."

"Hang on. There should be something in the bathing chamber."

Damn, Nyx could move fast. Almost before Pol could blink, he was back, waving a small container in triumph. Nyx flung himself back on the bed, handing his prize over. Pol turned it around in his hand, biting his lip. He wasn't entirely certain what to do with it. Oh, he had a general idea, but the application...

Nyx stole a kiss and took the container back. "I'll take care of it, *carissime*. You just keep touching me."

That, Pol could do.

Nyx sprawled out on his back and bent his knees. He gave Pol a little wink and popped the top off the oil. His expression was wicked as he dipped two fingers in. Pol bit his lip again and stroked Nyx's chest. He couldn't seem to move his eyes lower than his mate's nipples. They were very attractive, and Pol touched them, tweaking experimentally the way Nyx would sometimes do to him. Nyx's sound of approval was gratifying.

"You can look, Pol."

Pol wasn't certain he appreciated the amusement in Nyx's tone, but he still couldn't quite make himself move his eyes. Of all the times for that damned bashfulness to rear its annoying head...

Nyx was shifting against Pol in enticing ways, moans and groans of pleasure coming from him.

"Look, mate." He pressed a kiss to the side of Pol's neck. "Or better yet, feel."

Nyx grabbed one of Pol's hands. His touch was a little slimy from the oil, but warm and comforting. He guided Pol's fingers to his body, along his groin, bypassing his erection to that dark, hidden place. It felt so decadent to Pol, and a little naughty. His fingers brushed the back of Nyx's balls, drawing another strangled sound of pleasure.

Then he was there, feeling Nyx's fingers sliding in and out of his hole, slippery with oil, the skin soft and supple.

Shyness be damned. Pol had to see what he was feeling. He looked down and almost choked.

Oh, gods, that was... Well, he wasn't really certain what it was, besides incredibly erotic. Nyx had three of his long fingers buried in his arse, moving in and out in a slow, gentle rhythm.

Preparing himself for Pol's cock.

The thought had Pol reaching almost frantically for the aforementioned body part, grasping his erection firmly at the base to try to stave off the blast of lust that almost had him spilling his seed.

"Not yet," Nyx ordered. "I need you inside me first."

"I can..." Pol gasped, struggling for control. "I can go again."

"I don't want to wait."

Nyx pulled his fingers free and grabbed Pol, maneuvering him into place on top of him. The manhandling ratcheted Pol's arousal even higher. He clutched at Nyx's arms to steady himself.

"Take me," Nyx urged. "Claim me, as I claim you."

"I want that, so very much."

Pol did his best to straddle Nyx's hips, which suddenly seemed impossibly wide. He wiggled, Nyx groaning and cursing underneath him. He settled between Nyx's legs, the heat from the dragon almost scorching. Everywhere he touched, he hit scales.

"Control, Nyx," he said. "You're getting kind of sharp and scratchy."

"Sorry." Nyx squeezed his eyes closed, fighting to keep his human shape. Some of the scales receded, and the heat died down to a more bearable level.

"Thank you." Pol pressed his lips to the center of Nyx's chest, placing a small series of kisses, then beginning to suck up a mark.

"No more play," Nyx said. "Pol, please."

"You don't have to beg."

In truth, Pol was at a bit of a loss again. Luckily, Nyx was short on patience. He reached between them and used his long arms to guide Pol's cock between the cheeks of his arse. The tip slipped in, and Pol gasped. He'd never felt anything like it.

He moved, slowly and tentatively. Nyx clearly didn't like that. He spanned Pol's butt with his hands and tugged. Pol slipped in, the way made easy by the liberal application of oil and Nyx's large fingers.

"Oh!" Pol's shout of delight rang throughout the room. It went almost unheard, buried as it was beneath Nyx's ear-shattering roar.

The door crashed open, two armored guards bursting in with swords drawn, scanning for threats.

Nyx roared again. "Out!"

One of the guards turned bright red. They both exited as quickly as they could, tripping over each other to the loud clash of metal.

Pol started laughing. "Goddess, this place."

Nyx clearly didn't see the humor. He was snarling, eyes blazing, pupils slit until they almost disappeared in the green glow of his irises.

"Easy, mate," Pol soothed, touching his chest. He moved experimentally.

Yep, that did it. Nyx's attention immediately refocused on Pol.

"That's right. Look at me. We're not done yet, huh?"

Pol was suddenly feeling a surge of confidence. He didn't know where it had come from, but he wasn't about to question it. He slid his cock almost out, then plunged back in. Nyx's body swallowed him up, the grip tight sending sensations shooting up his spine. Wonderful sensations, like nothing he had ever felt before.

Nyx bellowed some more. Hopefully, the guards had passed the word and they wouldn't have any more interruptions. Not that Pol blamed them because, really, it sounded like someone was being murdered in here.

It was thrilling, knowing he could work his big, powerful dragon into such a frenzy.

Pol moved again, savoring the slip and slide, the way Nyx's body sucked him back in every time he tried to leave. Nyx gripped Pol's hips tightly. He would have bruises later, not that he cared. Using the hold, Nyx began moving Pol more quickly. Pol didn't even try to fight the superior strength of his mate and let himself be moved. He picked up the pace, helping out. He almost slipped sideways, and as he did, his cock brushed against something deep inside Nyx that pulled another roar out of the dragon.

"Oooh, you liked that."

"Mate." Nyx's voice was garbled, human speech beginning to desert him.

Pol got a faster rhythm going, one clearly more to Nyx's liking. Their skin slapped together steadily, pants and moans filling the air, punctuated by growls and snarls. Pol wasn't going to last much longer. Each plunge sent sparks through the head of his cock. His balls were tight and aching. His stomach rubbed against Nyx's rock-hard erection, the tip smearing pre-cum along his skin with wet warmth.

Nyx roared again. His body was shaking. He reared up, and there was nothing human about his gaze. Before Pol had a chance to panic, Nyx struck. He dug his fangs into the skin above Pol's heart. Pol yelled at the flash of pain. It only lasted a minute, then he could swear his veins caught on fire. He struggled in Nyx's hold, but the dragon wouldn't let him go.

The fire flared brighter then subsided into a dull heat that lit him from the inside out. Pol gasped. Everything in his body went tight, and the pleasure hit him with the force of a rogue ocean wave. He yelled again as his climax ripped him apart, only vaguely aware of Nyx's own bellow of release.

The sensations seemed to last an eternity, ecstasy battering at his body until it was nearly painful. Pol clung to Nyx, the only solid thing in a world gone red.

One last shudder, and Pol collapsed on top of Nyx. He felt drained, exhausted.

And utterly, completely sated.

"Great Goddess," he whispered, once could speak again. Although, his voice came out hoarse and weak. "I don't know that I want to do that again."

Nyx's laugh was equally weak. He patted Pol between the shoulders. "Won't be that intense next time."

"Good. Because I think doing that again would probably kill me."

"Me, too."

They lay there, sticky and sweaty, the position slightly uncomfortable, but neither had any inclination to move. Nyx placed a kiss on top of Pol's head.

"Mate." He sounded happy, possessive, and very pleased with himself.

"You did good."

The problems and worries of earlier seemed far away. In that moment, Pol felt untouchable. He was Nyx's, and the dragon wouldn't let anything happen.

Pol drifted off to sleep, cuddled close to his mate, more content than he had ever been in his life.

Chapter Fourteen

The note sat on Seamus' desk, innocuous in its plain envelope. There was nothing innocuous about its contents, however. The words seemed burned into his eyes. Coming into the room last night, seeing Nyx wrapped around a Pixie—that had been problem enough. Seamus had nothing against the Pixies as a race, but he preferred it when they stayed far from the capital. As they preferred that too, there typically wasn't any cause for concern.

But a Pixie and a Siren...he couldn't even imagine what that combination could do. He had visions of sundering mountains and boiling seas. Seamus rubbed the bridge of his nose. The problems never stopped anymore. What was it humans said? *I need a vacation.*

Unfortunately, as Desmond had pointed out, kings didn't get vacations, no matter how much they might need them.

"Majesty."

"Damn it."

"Well, good morning to you, too," Desmond replied dryly. He set the tea service down and surveyed Seamus with a frown. As usual, the steward looked impeccable. Seamus knew he, himself, was a touch on the rumpled side. That's what happened when you spent half the night up pacing.

"Did you know?" Seamus demanded.

"I believe I might have missed part of this conversation."

"About Pol. Did you know?"

"Since I have no idea what you are referring to, I'm going to go with 'no'."

"He's a halfling."

"Oh, then I can change my answer to yes. And perhaps you need glasses. I believe the fact that he's only half pixie is fairly obvious to anyone who looks. A relief, for certain, as he doesn't display any other worrying characteristics. Human, perhaps, on the other side? The size certainly —"

"Siren." Seamus interrupted the rambling flow of words. "The other half is Siren."

That shut Desmond up quickly. "Siren?" he asked uncertainly. "Are you positive? I have never heard of those races mixing."

"For damned good reason." Seamus began to pace, the nervous energy needing an outlet. "And if I had known... But damn it, he's a dragon mate now. I can't touch him."

"Majesty!"

"Don't give me that look, Desmond." Seamus knew he sounded uncaring, but the simple fact was, Pol presented a real danger to the balance of power in Faerie. He was a threat to Seamus, and if Seamus had known about Pol's birth, the half-Pixie, half-Siren boy would not have survived to be a man. Maybe that made him cruel, but combining the magic of the Sirens and the magic of the Pixies...Seamus had worked too hard, for too long, to let someone take everything apart.

"Seamus—"

"Fuck this." He rarely used the F-word—it was a very human thing to do—but it seemed appropriate for the moment. "I'm going to take a walk. Don't disturb me for the next couple of hours."

Seamus couldn't stay still any longer, and he certainly didn't want to continue this particular conversation. There was no point. It would only irritate him.

He left Desmond behind, the poor man still stammering, and made for the nearest exit.

The gods take it. He wondered how much panic would be stirred up if he disappeared for a few days.

* * * *

Desmond sighed. "You heard?" he asked without turning around.

Raven came up behind him. Seamus had been so agitated, he had never even noticed the man's presence.

"I heard. Do I need to send Nyx and Pol back to Benndragos? King or not, I cannot allow—"

Desmond shook his head. "No. Perhaps if they had not yet mated, but he won't risk losing one of the Draak. There are too few of you already, and you're going to be needed."

Raven gave Desmond a sharp look. "Is that prophecy or speculation?"

"A little of both, I believe."

Raven sighed. "I cannot say I'm sorry, because I'm not. I can feel the strength in Pol. He will make a most excellent addition to our world."

"Can you assure me, beyond a doubt, that he isn't a threat?"

Desmond peered intently at Raven, willing him to give an answer they could all live with. Raven's dark blue eyes went cloudy for a moment, the dragon staring at something only he could see.

"Yes," finally came the low, gravelly answer. "Yes, I can assure you he is an asset, not a threat. There is no ambition in the man."

Desmond heaved a sigh of relief. "Now, if I can only get Seamus to accept that."

"He must. Because I will not allow my dragons to go into an extended slumber if I cannot ensure the safety of the mates left behind."

"Raven—"

"No."

Desmond damn near took a step back at the sharp tone. Raven's gaze, when it turned his way, was ice cold, those blue eyes freezing him to the core.

"Peace, Desmond. I am not angry with you," Raven assured.

One large hand dropped onto Desmond's shoulder, and Raven gave a little squeeze. Knowing how rare it was for the dragon leader to touch anyone aside from the other dragons, Desmond accepted it as the apology it was.

"It's frustrating, is all. One would think that, after all these millennia, Seamus would have learnt to trust me."

"He doe—"

"No, he doesn't."

Raven's eyes were sad now, and Desmond wanted to go find their king and give him a swift kick in the hind end. The man forgot, sometimes, that he wasn't alone.

"It is my duty to keep our king safe, and I will do so, as I have always done. The Pixie is not a threat."

Raven turned and left, the huge form silent. Desmond watched him go, the strength in the man palpable. He sighed again.

"I believe it is time to have a nice, long discussion with our king."

Then he needed to make some arrangements. Tempers always flared when they had put The Renewal off for too long. They were all feeling the strain.

He found Seamus precisely where he'd expected. The king stood at the highest point in the palace, staring out over the land. Most of the royal residence was built in an Eastern style, long and low, but there were a few hints of Western architecture in the outer walls and the inclusion of two large towers. The one on the north end was the largest, and from the top parapet a person could see for miles. That was so long as they didn't mind the open walls and the low stone half-wall being the only barrier between them and a very long fall.

Seamus had one foot braced atop said barrier, oblivious to any danger. He stood with his hand clutching one of the roof supports. His eyes were fixed on the horizon. From here, the hazy mounds of the mountains were barely visible as they rose above the landscape. Those mountains formed the backbone of the continent, bisecting the land in the center before curving to follow the coastline. While the dragons had claimed a large majority for themselves, the northernmost portions of the mountain range still held many secrets. Not even magic could penetrate some of the more remote passes and valleys.

Desmond knew them all well. Both the mountains, and the secrets. Perhaps it was time to remind Seamus of that little fact.

"I know. I'm overreacting," Seamus said before Desmond had the chance to speak.

"It's always nice to be aware of your flaws."

"Of which I have many, according to you."

Desmond sighed. "I understand that you're wary of the power Pol would be able to wield. I'm wary of it, too. Any sensible person would be."

"I hear the 'but' coming."

"Indeed. When the personality is not yet formed, when there is still a chance of a threat, I might have agreed with more...drastic measures. But Pol is grown, albeit still very, very young. His personality is set, and I see no danger in it. Raven is convinced, and his conviction has, in turn, convinced *me*."

"My sole purpose in life is to keep the people of this realm safe," Seamus said, a hint of anger entering his voice. "I cannot do that if my closest allies keep—"

"You're looking at this the wrong way," Desmond interrupted, with some anger of his own.

"Am I?" For the first time, Seamus turned to look at him. Desmond wouldn't admit it aloud, but the king's position on the wall was starting to make him nervous, especially once he turned his attention away from the view.

"You are," Desmond said.

"Do enlighten me."

The sarcasm in the king's voice was the final irritant. "*Petsi!*"

The curse took Seamus aback, and he finally looked at Desmond. Or rather, he finally looked and *saw*.

"Desmond—"

"Shut up. I'm speaking now." Desmond let out a low string of very obscure, very old imprecations. Seamus showed uncharacteristic patience and restraint, and remained silent.

"I'm going to put this in a way you would best understand, since you seem to be caught in a threat-analysis mode."

"You've been reading books from Earth again."

"Be silent. According to you at the moment, people of power are either a threat or an asset. Raven assures me that Pol is not a threat, which automatically makes him an asset."

Seamus opened his mouth then closed it again. A thoughtful look crossed his face. Unfortunately, it was soon replaced by a scowl.

"But the threat will always remain. Buried, perhaps, but there."

"I suggest you listen to the advice of your people." A new voice entered the conversation. Desmond smiled.

Now, perhaps, the king could be made to see reason.

With well-honed discretion, Desmond made his retreat, leaving Seamus to the care and attention of General Marius Mtalna.

Chapter Fifteen

"I would like to officially welcome you to the palace, Pol de Maldra. May your mating be long and prosperous."

The words were gracious, the tone even. But the eyes...the king was not happy, not one little bit. Desmond, standing a few paces to one side, looked annoyed. A burly bearded man near Desmond looked equal parts exasperated and amused. Nyx was scowling.

Cody was scowling too, and Pol found him more frightening than any dragon. The dragons were blustery. Cody was not.

I hope he isn't armed.

After that grudging announcement, Seamus ignored Pol. That was fine by Pol. Unnoticed and ignored. That was his preferred situation.

The small room seemed crowded with the large forms of all the dragons stuffed into it. They looked decidedly out of place amongst the delicate furniture and flowered cushions. Desmond had called it the small receiving room when he had summoned Nyx and Pol. They should have used the large receiving room.

"We're going to have a lot of fun."

Pol turned, startled, to find Cody at his side. The other dragon mate looked far too pleased for Pol's peace of mind.

"I've been going nuts trying to deal with these idiots all by myself," Cody continued. "It will be nice to have some back-up."

I'm going to back up all right. Why the heck hadn't Nyx mentioned that Cody was part demon? His eyes certainly glinted like one. It was making Pol nervous.

He bit his lip and tracked Nyx's movements. The dragons were deep in conversation on the other side of the room. It was too far away for Pol's peace of mind.

Someone knocked on the door. Pol wouldn't have minded the interruption, except the page was blocking his path. Pol still hadn't ruled out needing to make a hasty exit.

"You have visitors, Majesty," the page announced.

Seamus smiled. Pol went from biting his lip to chewing on it. He didn't trust that smile. *Damn it, Nyx.* Why hadn't they followed through with Nyx's escape plan last night?

"Please show them in," Seamus said, still with that smile — almost a smirk, really — still on his sharp features.

The page bowed, then ushered in a group of far too familiar people. Pol couldn't help it. He let out a rare but heartfelt curse.

"I take it you know them," Cody said.

"Unfortunately, yes. The old, pretentious ones are the Pixie elders. The sullen one is my cousin, Paul."

"Pol and Paul?" Cody snorted.

"Our parents thought it would be cute." Pol still shook his head at the delusions suffered by both parties. "They had grand visions of a marriage alliance. Can you see it? Pol and Paul Petri."

"Oh, God." Cody doubled over in laughter, earning a glare from the newcomers. Pol admired the way Cody didn't even seem to notice.

"I know," Pol said. "They were all nuts. I would have refused him on his name alone. The fact that he's a total idiot only made it easier."

The elders began to make their way to the king. Pol didn't like how self-satisfied they appeared, but there wasn't much he could do about it. To his surprise, Paul crossed the room to stand next to him.

"What are you doing?" Pol asked.

Paul looked, if possible, even more sullen. "Look, I don't like you. I think you're a stuck up little prick."

Look who's talking.

"But I don't want to see you hurt, and the elders aren't playing nice any more. So, for what it's worth, I'll support you in this. You may be an idiot and a pushover—"

"Wow, thanks."

"—but you're family, and you're the Duke. They don't have the right to take that away."

"You're a duke?" Cody sounded impressed.

"I don't want it," Pol said. "It's a lot of work, a lot of trouble, and the elders think it's a free pass to meddle in every minute aspect of your life. I wish..."

Pol trailed off as an idea occurred to him. He narrowed his eyes, studying his cousin from a new perspective.

Paul looked the same as always. He was tall for a Pixie, almost five foot seven, and stick-skinny. His features were angular, his dark green eyes deep-set and a touch small for his face. His matching dark green hair was cut uncharacteristically short, and it wasn't the best look for him. It stuck up in messy, uneven spikes. Pol wondered if he cut it himself. With a dull knife.

But there was intelligence in those beady eyes. And Paul was right—they were blood, and for Pixies, that meant something. Family ties were important.

It didn't take long for Pol to come to a decision, and really, it was a wonder he hadn't thought of it before. Really, he could be an idiot sometimes. The elders may have decided that Paul wasn't a suitable candidate for the duchy, but the elders weren't the only ones who could make that decision.

"Paul."

Paul turned his attention to Pol. Across the room, the elders were speaking in low voices with the king. A worried Desmond hovered nearby. The only sound Pol could make out with clarity was Nyx's low growl. Raven had one hand on Nyx's shoulder, but he, too, was glaring at the small gathering.

He had best work quickly.

"They're going to come to an agreement soon about the duchy," Pol said. "And it's not going to make anyone happy."

"Probably not," Paul agreed. "They've been talking joint rule and frankly, I don't think it's going to work."

"Not to mention joint rule means the elders," Pol mused aloud. "And I don't trust them to do what's best for nature over what's best for the Pixies." *Or themselves.*

Pol stuck out his hand. Paul still had his attention focused on the meeting, or else he wouldn't have clasped it. His body was operating automatically while his brain was otherwise engaged. Pol took advantage, clasping Paul's arm above the wrist. Paul looked alarmed and tried to pull away, but Pol wouldn't let him.

He cleared his throat, feeling the weight of unfriendly gazes at the sound. "Paul Petri," he declared loudly. "I, Pol de Maldra, fourth Duke of Penoply, name you my heir, henceforth to act in my stead and with the full power of the magic and lineage."

"Wait, what—?"

"Accept," Pol said in a low voice. "Now, damn it."

"I... This is... Fine, you bastard." Paul glared, but dutifully replied, "I, Paul Petri, do so accept the rights and responsibilities as your heir."

Pol felt the magic buzzing under his skin, the ties of his heritage waking. Looking sideways, Pol grinned at the wide-eyed elders. This was rather fun.

Paul tried again to pull away, but Pol kept holding on. He dug deep inside, searching for the link that bound him not only to the position of Duke, but to the forest of Elithorn. He coaxed and cajoled, bending the magic to his will. It responded sluggishly, until he pointed it in the direction of his cousin. Then it perked up, like a puppy spotting its new owner, and surged to the surface. Magic crackled and popped, sending little shafts of electricity arcing along his skin.

Paul yelped.

"I hereby renounce my claim to the title of Penoply," Pol said. "Rule wisely, Paul Petri, fifth Duke of Penoply."

One of the elders shouted. Pol was too busy to respond. Pol held onto his cousin, Paul's grip tightening in return. Magic pooled between them at the connection of their hands in visible swirls, a rainbow of colors that leaped and danced as the power passed from one member of the bloodline to another. It took mere seconds for the transfer to be completed, and when it was, Pol let go with a grateful sigh. He flexed his hand, fingers aching.

"You really are a bastard." Paul stared with hard, angry eyes.

Pol took a judicious step back, since it looked like his cousin wanted to haul off and hit him. Pol grinned. "Maybe. But I'm a common bastard, now, aren't I?"

"I hate you."

"Why? I just made you a duke."

"Congrats," Cody declared, slapping Paul on the shoulder and sending Paul reeling sideways. No one else seemed capable of reacting yet.

Then the unknown bearded man began to chuckle. "Very nice," he said. Pol had never heard a voice that deep — it seemed to rumble up from somewhere in the vicinity of the man's toes.

Desmond, clearly sensing an impending explosion, managed to adroitly maneuver the elders through a connecting door to the next room. Seamus stood. The look on his face was considering, but to Pol's relief, seemed to lack some of the earlier menace.

"Not many men would give up claim to a role that is one step from royalty."

"I'm not most men," Pol admitted. He looked to Nyx. Satisfaction filled him when Nyx swiftly crossed the room to take his hand. "I have everything I need right here," Pol continued. "I have a cozy little house, a lovely garden to play in, and my mate to love. I don't need power or wealth to be happy, and I never have. It certainly didn't make my parents happy. I want a family and a normal life."

"You're mated to a dragon," Cody said dryly. "A normal life isn't in the cards."

Pol shrugged. "It's normal enough for me. I'm a lazy person at heart. Power is too much work."

The big bearded man started to laugh then covered it up with a quick cough when Seamus glared at him. He shrugged too, but it looked more impressive considering the breadth of the man's shoulders. "I like him. He's got a good sense of humor. It's a positive sign. You ever met a power-hungry, potential villain with a sense of humor?"

With a sigh, Seamus shook his head. Then his mouth twitched. "I know when I've been bested," he said. "Congratulations on your mating."

This time, he sounded sincere.

"Thank you, Your Majesty." Pol could be gracious, too. Even if the king still made him nervous. He would probably never be comfortable around Seamus. First impressions tended to stick.

"Well, that was settled nicely," Cody declared. "We should have a party to celebrate or something. But none of your balls, Seamus. They're deadly dull."

"I'm afraid there won't be time." There was genuine regret in Seamus' voice and on his face. "The last of the arrangements have been made. I'm dismissing you all from duty as of this moment. Enjoy your evening, because tomorrow, we begin The Renewal."

Chapter Sixteen

The moonlight called to Pol, as loud and piercing as the screeching of a flock of seagulls. And Goddess, why was he thinking of the ocean again? He could hear it, mixing with the moonlight's song, the rhythmic crash of waves resonating deep inside him, steady as the rush of blood.

Pol tossed back the covers and stood, grabbing the nearest bit of fabric. It turned out to be Nyx's robe, and it completely swathed him from head to toe, but he wouldn't be wearing it long, anyway. He needed the moons. Now. The moons, and the plants, and dirt beneath his feet.

Damnation. He must have woken something inside himself earlier today, because he had never felt so overwhelmed by his magic before.

Pol slipped from the room, leaving a sleeping Nyx behind. His dragon would wake soon and follow, no doubt. Ever since their official mating, the connection had grown. It wouldn't take long for Nyx to feel his absence. Until then, Pol would let him sleep. This wasn't something the dragon could help with, anyway.

His bare feet made no sound as he crossed the hallway and down the stairs. Each patch of light spilling through open windows increased the call. It was the Siren part of him, Pol imagined. Most Pixies were all about the sun, but for Pol, night had always held the biggest attraction. The air itself smelled different after midnight, fresher, more soothing.

The kitchen door swung closed behind Pol as he stepped outside, taking a deep breath. Tension he hadn't known he'd been carrying slipped away with every inhale. The hum of nature grew louder in his ears, melding with the *shush* of unseen waves.

Pol took the path deeper into the garden. Leaves and branches stretched to reach for him as he passed, and he gave them all a gentle caress in greeting. In the center of his tiny bit of paradise, the glow of the moons poured down, the fountain shining brilliantly white in the reflected light.

Pol began humming. The city lay still and silent in the pre-dawn hours. Too late for the night owls, too soon for the early risers. Perfect.

The trickling of water from the fountain grew louder as he drew closer, not only from proximity. The flow increased until the usually small tendrils became a cascade flowing from the top and splashing merrily into the pool. Pol dropped the robe, relishing the feel of the cool air brushing against his naked skin. He stepped over the lip of the fountain into the pool and embraced the water, letting the hum grow into a song.

It was an old lullaby, familiar to any child, but its age lent it a power that was often overlooked. Pol let the words pour out, and with it, his magic.

Trees creaked and groaned, birds took flight, and over the rush of water and the melody of his song, Pol heard the loud rustling of leaves.

This. This was why a Pixie hybrid was feared. This was why *Pol* was feared.

All around him, nature burst to life. To his right, a sapling shot toward the sky, trunk thickening and roots burrowing through the dirt. Its power spread to the wall then beyond, splitting the stone barrier as if it were sand. The ground vibrated with the force of life.

Pol stood at the center of it all, his lullaby melding into a ballad then a joyous hymn of celebration. Water cascaded around him, plastering his hair to his skin. He blinked as it forced his eyes closed, then left them that way.

This was all internal. He didn't need to see.

A presence entered his garden, solid and strong. Old. Powerful. Comforting. It felt like the presence of the Willow or the ancient oaks of his homeland.

Pol blinked his eyes opened and smiled, spreading his arms in welcome.

"What are you doing, *carissime*?" Nyx asked. A smile flirted around his eyes.

"Celebrating. Come join me."

To Pol's utter shock, Nyx did. Still clothed in a hastily drawn on pair of pants, he stepped into the fountain and pulled Pol into his arms.

"Show me," he whispered.

Pol began singing again, the warmth of his mate's embrace grounding him. Together they watched as the garden bloomed, color spreading through the greenery. More trees stretched to the sky, maturing under the power of Pol's magic. The power of life.

It might have been minutes, or it might have been hours, when Pol's songs finally ran dry. The flow of the fountain decreased. In the east, the sky was beginning to lighten with the approaching sunrise.

"The power of life, indeed."

Pol jerked, almost slipping. Only Nyx's secure grip kept him from tumbling headfirst into the water lapping around his ankles.

Seamus stepped out of the shadows, and Pol winced, although really, he should have expected it. With the amount of power he'd been putting out...well, of course he was going to attract the king's attention.

Nyx tightened his hold, growling at the monarch.

"Peace, Nyx." Seamus frowned. Pol didn't think he was imagining the hurt in the expression. "I understand your reaction, but I'm not here to hurt him. I only wanted to see."

Pol patted Nyx, then carefully climbed out of the fountain. The last thing he needed was for his natural clumsiness to manifest and send him toppling. He grabbed up Nyx's robe and wrapped it around his nude body. It wasn't until the displeased rumble stopped that Pol understood Nyx had been unhappy about his unclothed state.

"I have no interest in your mate, Nyx," Seamus said with amusement. "No need to get jealous."

"He is for my eyes only," Nyx said around a snarl.

"Of course, of course." Seamus strode a few yards down the path, examining Pol's newly expanded garden. "This is quite well done, little one. A beautiful display."

"I... Thank you, Your Majesty." Pol wasn't certain what to say, or how to feel. Only yesterday, the power behind that 'beautiful display' had put his life in danger from this man. Now he was giving out compliments?

Seamus sighed. He stared at the ground for a moment. "I owe you both an apology, but most especially you, Nyx. You've been at my side for many years, and your loyalty has never been in question. I should not have done so now. I should have trusted you, should have trusted in the bond between mates. Your character would never allow for a connection between someone who would cause our world harm. I forgot that briefly, and I deeply regret it."

When Pol looked, he saw Nyx's mouth literally hanging open. He suspected it was the first time the dragon had ever heard his king apologize.

"Thank you, Seamus," Nyx said when he could speak again.

"I just need you both to understand that while Pol's power is beautiful, it is potent."

And here comes the lecture. Pol had known it would be in there somewhere.

"The opposite side of life is death," Seamus continued. "While Pol's power can bring such a magnificent display of growth and rebirth, it can also spur destruction and death. I have a duty to my people, to protect them from harm to the best of my ability."

"In practical terms, what are you trying to say?" Nyx demanded.

Seamus finally looked up. He smiled. "Nothing, actually. I would ask Pol to exercise caution and discretion regarding his abilities. That's all. His magic is a gift, and there are always those willing to exploit such a gift."

"That's why he has me," Nyx said. He crossed his arms over his powerful chest. Pol found him magnificent and couldn't resist stepping closer to touch. Nyx's hard features softened when Pol's fingers brushed against his skin. He dropped his arms and took Pol's hand, giving it a little squeeze. "It is my honor and pleasure to protect him and shelter him from any who wish to use him for ill."

"So formal, my dragon." Seamus chuckled softly.

Nyx shrugged. "As you say, I'm a dragon."

"You're my dragon," Pol said.

"Not to change the subject," Seamus said, obviously doing just that. "But I did have one request. I would prefer it, Pol, if you would come and stay at the palace while the dragons are...indisposed."

Nyx's eyes narrowed and he began growling again. "You believe there's still danger?"

"I need someone to keep Cody occupied."

Alarm speared through Pol. "Majesty, I'm not certain—"

"I'm not asking you to keep him out of trouble," Seamus clarified. "No one can manage that. Just try to keep him from beating up any more of my nobility."

Maybe if Pol begged, Seamus would put him to sleep with the dragons.

Epilogue

It was an actual cave. Cody shouldn't be surprised by now and yet, he always was. He supposed he could blame it on his upbringing—or rather, where his upbringing had occurred. He was far more used to Earth's concrete and steel than Faerie's rock and dirt.

As far as caves went, Cody supposed it was nice enough. Not homey, like the dragon caves, but it was certainly impressive. The roof towered a half-mile overhead, open in the middle to allow a thick shaft of sunlight to illuminate the pale gray stone with a warm hue. The sun hit the floor in an almost perfect circle, and someone had clearly planned for that, as it highlighted the circular mosaic on the floor. Cody took a step closer, but the images made no sense to him. Lots of fire and hazy figures.

At the far end of the cave was a massive altar, a set of three steps leading to it. Seamus was already there, paging through the largest book Cody had ever seen. He hoped they never moved it, because it would take at least four people to carry. On either side, surrounding the circle in a large U, was a dozen or so…well, the only thing Cody could call them was beds, but considering they were made of the same rock that lined the cave walls, he didn't think they really deserved the name. They were gorgeous, elaborately carved with symbols and runes that probably had a great deal of significance, although Cody remained clueless. Raven was already sitting on one, stretching, preparing for his long nap.

Cody scowled at their surroundings. It was all so ceremonial. Cold, ritualistic and intimidating. Would it have hurt to give the dragons somewhere lush and comfortable to stay? After all, they were going to be trapped here for almost two months. An actual bed would have been nice.

Cody said something to that effect, and Kirit almost grinned — almost. His dragon was too upset about the current situation for true amusement.

"We'll be unconscious," he said. "Comfort isn't a concern."

"There is a reason," Seamus called across the room, not looking up from his perusal. "The center of the 'beds' are quartz, which makes an excellent magical conductor."

"Plus, this way, there will be no collapsing or destruction if one of us goes dragon while sleeping," Chaos interjected wryly.

"Got it." Ask a simple question, get a lecture. Cody was growing accustomed to it. Didn't make it any less annoying, though.

Chaos hopped up onto one of the altars, wiggling his butt on the stone. "Marvelous," he declared. "I shall be as comfortable as a babe in a cradle."

"Just think," Cody said to no one in particular. "Two whole months without *him*. I'm not going to know how to handle the silence."

"Admit it. You'll miss me!"

"Like a toothache." He would.

Kirit hadn't let go of his tight grip on Cody's hand since they'd left the palace. Cody, for his part, was finding it difficult to look at the big dragon. Emotions were not his thing, especially mushy emotions. This event practically screamed for mushy emotions.

"Mate."

Reluctantly, Cody stopped examining their surroundings and looked up into Kirit's eyes.

"'Twill be fine, mate." One side of Kirit's mouth tilted up in the barest hints of a smile. "The time will pass quickly, and I will return before you can miss me."

"Not possible." Cody had to stand on his tiptoes to press his palm against Kirit's cheek. Kirit turned his head and placed a small kiss in the center. "I miss you already."

"And I, you. Stay safe."

For once Cody didn't protest as Kirit took a grip on his waist and hoisted him into the air. He tangled his fingers in Kirit's long, thick hair and kissed him, trying to infuse it with all the love and longing he felt.

When Kirit lowered him to the ground, they were both trembling and hard. For an instant, Kirit's eyes glinted with familiar wicked humor.

"Something to remember me by," he said. "And to give you something to look forward to."

"Jerk," Cody said fondly. He sniffled, but it was only the damp air in the cave. And his eyes most definitely weren't stinging.

"I love you, too," Kirit said. One last caress, and he stepped away. Cody watched him take his place in the circle and wanted nothing more than to curl up next to the dragon.

"Nyx," Seamus called. "Please take your place. We are ready to begin."

Lost in his own misery, Cody had completely forgotten about the other couple. He felt an unaccustomed twinge of guilt. Two months without Kirit was bad enough, but poor Pol. Their relationship was so new.

Nyx brushed past him, looking thoroughly miserable. Cody walked toward the entrance to stand next to Pol. He took the small Pixie's hand and gave it a little squeeze.

He didn't try to say anything comforting, even when he heard the hitch in Pol's breath.

It's only two months, he told himself yet again as Seamus began to chant. *Hardly any time at all in the long run.*

No matter how many times he said it, though, it never helped.

About the Author

Born and raised in the middle of the Midwest, I have always been a dreamer. More often than not I could be found with my nose buried in a book (many of which I had to sneak past my parents). It wasn't long before I started trying my hand at writing more of the stories I loved. After years of penning tales that rarely left the hard drive of my computer, I discovered M/M romance. As with all genres, it wasn't long before my own characters started to take shape.

There is little I love more than wandering new places and, on occasion, entirely new worlds with my characters. They can range from cowboys to Victorian noblemen, accountants to shapeshifters, and everything in between. I write mainly m/m romance, usually with paranormal or fantasy elements. I willingly follow my characters wherever they decide to go, sometimes with unusual results. I have little control over their actions—any naughty behaviour is all their doing!

KM Mahoney loves to hear from readers. You can find her contact information, website details and author profile page at http://www.totallybound.com.

Totally Bound Publishing